MacIan's Gift
Tartan Threads Book One

by

Terry Graham

MacIan's Gift

Contact Information: info@thewildrosepress.com

Cover Art by *Diana Carlile*

The Wild Rose Press, Inc.
PO Box 708
Adams Basin, NY 14410-0708

Visit us at www.thewildrosepress.com

Publishing History
First Edition, 2021

Print ISBN 978-1-5092-3924-5
Digital ISBN 978-1-5092-3925-2
Published in the United States of America

**The gift of love and family
can be found where you least expect it.**

"Please," the would-be ghost begged, in French. "I don't want to hurt you."

A second later, a scream erupted, deafening and shrill. Jamie lunged forward. Something crashed into him, arms and legs flailing. The taper hurtled to the ground. Carson cursed, and Jamie's shin exploded with pain. When another shape slammed against him, his sword hand smashed into the wall. His weapon clanged against the stone.

With a calculated swipe, Jamie reached out. His fingers latched onto thin bone and locked. He hauled it close, latching an arm about the small frame. Another frightened wail raised hackles on his neck. Tiny hands and feet pummeled him, like a barrage of snowballs thrown by weaklings, constant but harmless. His captive wrenched free. He surged forward. A form collapsed beneath him, bony and wet. A whoosh of air burst in his face, but as he reached out, the figure slipped away. A scrambling noise directed him to the right. With a final burst of speed, he wrapped his arms around a writhing form.

"No!" A wrenching sob tore the air. Tiny hands locked onto his arms, scratching and pushing to no avail. He tightened the embrace, lifting the form from the ground. Feet thrashed at his thighs, one lucky swing connecting with his nutmegs.

He sucked in a breath and held tighter. Terror soaked into him. Frail ribs heaved beneath icy skin; raspy panicked breaths beat at him. The entire form shook.

"Ack, *aon bheag*," he whispered as a curly head banged at his neck and chest. "I'll not hurt ye."

Dedication

To my son, my own gift from the heavens.

Chapter One

Scottish Trossachs, Spring 1651

"Have ye been praying, child?"

As soon as Sarah Clinton raised her eyelids, she realized she was in trouble. Her stepfather's eyes flashed like black obsidian, darker even than the cold cramped study. Short and burly, Hammond Mitchell ruled his castle through intimidation and cruelty, a fact she'd learned early on in her mother's marriage to the dour Scotsman. Despite his stature, he towered over her kneeling form, one hand stroking the affliction that nestled beneath his plaid kilt. As she watched, the mass swelled, telling her what she already suspected.

He planned to beat her again.

Desperate, her gaze circled the room. Heavy furniture crowded the space, the red velvet more black than scarlet and worn through from decades of use. In one corner sat Eilidh, Hammond's sister and her mother's longtime nurse. Gnarled hands clutched the leather straps used when Sarah's mother needed calming, slapping against the older woman's flabby thighs while a smirk twisted her paunchy face. Larger and more manly looking than her brother, Eilidh's methods of punishment were more subtle than Hammond's and just as effective.

With a shudder, Sarah's gaze wandered toward a

form in the corner. Beside the ratty brown curtains, Hammond's bastard son stared out the arrow slit window. Rain that hadn't let up for three days scurried down the grimy green glass. Taller and thinner than his father, Euanan qualified as a handsome man by most standards, but to Sarah, he was an unknown she feared even more than Hammond.

"Yes, sir." She choked the words past a lump of dread and lowered her gaze to the floor. "Three times a day." Just as he had decreed she should. Not the prayers he said she should lift to God, though. She didn't pray that her deeds pleased God or thank him for his grace. She prayed for salvation; a blessing Hammond believed few achieved. She prayed each time he sent for her; that he'd not beat her again, that her uncle might rescue her, that she'd escape the Hell they called Mitchell Castle.

"Sloth is a sin, child," he said, and she flinched, unable to prevent shrinking away from the hand he lifted. Calloused and rough, with one finger missing, his knuckle scraped the bruise he'd left two days earlier then slid along the edge of her plain linen kerchief. "I trust ye've been fighting it." His gaze flicked over her right leg, lips curling with disgust.

"Yes, sir." When he leaned closer, her stomach heaved, and she held her breath. A rancid garlic scent lingered in the air, along with another strange smell that increased whenever his affliction protruded. "I finished the mending, stripped the bed, and swept my bedroom floor." She'd wanted to lay new straw, but the straw they'd brought was moldy and stank. Even now, her weak leg screamed in protest at the work she'd done, her jaw and ribs still aching from the blows he'd administered for venturing from her room without permission.

"Just get on with it, Da." Euanan spun away from the window and marched toward the massive desk behind his father. He perched on one corner of the blackened wood, one wool-clad knee bent above his buckled shoe. Unlike Hammond's Scottish attire, he wore petticoat breeches and slashed sleeves crafted of the finest linen. A long blond wig accentuated midnight eyes that dominated his pale face.

Hammond's forehead crinkled as he turned toward his son.

"Are ye sure ye want to marry her? What if she's mad like her mother? She's dim-witted enough as 'tis, not to mention a cripple."

Sarah stomach heaved again, bile from the mealy breakfast porridge rising to burn her throat. Marry Euanan? She'd rather die.

"It matters not." Euanan's perfectly manicured fingers waved it away. "Snuff the candles, lift her legs, and she'll get a brat just as well as anyone else. We only need one, and it doesn't matter if it's an imbecile or not. Twill still be a Campbell."

Horror flooded Sarah, and she gaped at the two men. They were as insane as her mother.

"I suppose that's true." A feverish light lit Hammond's eyes, and a red-tipped tongue darted out. The look on his face sent shivers through her, like an army of millipedes crawling inside her. "And I can keep trying until she gets it right."

Euanan shrugged. "As you please. I care not as long as I don't have to do the deed."

Sarah's eyes widened. Euanan's lips curled with distaste and icy black eyes stabbed her. She'd heard the whispers. Despite two previous marriages, Euanan preferred the beds of men, if she understood the strange Gaelic words correctly. Both women had died soon after wedding him. Had they too been victims of Hammond's evil schemes?

"No!" The word slipped out, and both men frowned. "I won't marry you."

Hammond's hand lashed out and jerked Sarah's head back by her tight braid. "Ye'll do as ye're told, *Bruchag.*"

Witch. He'd called her a witch.

"My uncle will never allow it," she said, gritting her teeth against the burn in her scalp.

Euanan laughed and waved a yellowed parchment. "Your uncle has already agreed. Refused to let Da have you, but he agreed to me. Said no one else wanted a cripple."

Stunned, Sarah's hope crumpled. She'd written to her uncle every day since her mother had wed Hammond Mitchell. Every day she prayed he'd come rescue her. She should have known better.

Alexander Campbell had schooled her in the politics of the Highlands, drummed it into her every time he visited. *You're a Campbell, lass, and Campbells breed power.*

Her mother had been a Campbell, too. Despite a fragile mind, they had wed her to the wealthiest man in England. Then, after he died, Hammond married her. Hammond had beat her mother when Archibald Campbell, laird of the entire Campbell clan, said they wouldn't recognize the marriage. Hammond's subsequent refusal to send troops during the battle of Dunbar had resulted in the Campbell's worst defeat

4

ever. Her mother had died soon after.

Since then, Alexander had been trying to swell his uncle's forces. Hammond boasted men in the hundreds, a significant number.

A whimper escaped her. Hammond's mouth curved into a smile, and the pull on her hair released.

"That's a good lass," he said as she lurched to her hands and knees. The toe of his boot struck out, and a flash of agony seared through her ribs. "I'll only hurt ye a little. Have to make sure ye can stand up to speak the vows."

Sarah curled into a ball and held onto the one remaining truth.

She might be a cripple, but unless they killed her, she could still run.

****

"There it is, lads." Jamie MacIan reined in his mount and stared at the pile of stones peeking through the tree-tops while the rest of his group of rag-tag Scots crowned the last peak.

Set in a fold, the mountain formed one side of the small castle. The remnants of a square courtyard opened to a wide swath of green that ran the length of the mountain then dropped into a forest ravine shrouded in mist. A single tower stood sentinel, embracing the main keep. The other towers slumped on the ground like fallen warriors slain by the first. Behind the castle, the mountain rose in an incline so steep even sheep avoided it. The other side, Jamie had learned on earlier explorations, was nearly as steep.

It would take years to restore the entirety, but the main keep could be habitable before winter.

A restless excitement thrummed through his body

despite nine days of excruciatingly slow travel. It had taken ten years to realize his dream; ten years of saving every pound that crossed his palm. Now, the realization of that dream lay before him. A sliver of sun, the first they'd seen in three days, reflected off the dull stone as if in welcome.

"Looks like a pile of bones to me," Patrick said, with a laugh and a reassuring pat to his gray mount. Barely twenty, and his laird's youngest brother, Patrick's cheery nature had kept their spirits up during what had turned out to be one of the coldest, wettest journeys they'd ever made.

"I don't care if it's a pile of nettles. If it's dry, I'll lie in it." Another of his companions and his closest friend, Malcolm Grant threw back the edge of his tartan and stretched. Droplets of rain sparkled in his umber beard, shaken loose as his massive form shuddered.

"I ken it's not much," Jamie admitted while he scanned the remainder of the group. A mere ten in total, eight stared back as if awaiting orders, just as he had always stared back at his laird, Bryan MacGregor. Aside from Rory, the youngest, he trusted each one with his life and would give his in a heartbeat. With luck and a tremendous amount of work, he vowed he'd give them the life they sought. "It's ours though. The land's fertile, there are four small streams running through it, with pike, salmon, and trout, and the mountains can support enough sheep to clothe ourselves–"

"Ack, shut yer gob, Jamie." An older man pushed his horse through and spat a wad of tobacco out. "Tis a fine tract. Just needs a bit o' work. Won't get done if we sit and gab, though." Without waiting for a response, Jock picked his way along a deer trail that led off to the right. One by one the others followed. A quiet murmur of excitement replaced the grumbling that had settled over them.

Within an hour, the tower soared above them, the square courtyard reaching out broken arms in welcome. Pieces of wall scattered the ground. Roots and trees cracked much of the structure, hiding the white stone that had lain neglected for too long.

Jamie bounced from his horse and dropped the reins, unable to suppress the smile that split his face.

"Your granny would be pleased," Malcolm said as his hand ran along a twisted length of iron. The remnants of a gate bar, the metal twisted amidst bits of charred wood. Malcolm's blue eyes scanned the ruins with an approving nod. "She'll be a beauty once we're done."

"Do ye think Lady Aalis is here?" Patrick asked with a mischievous grin.

Young Rory's brown eyes widened with the look of a frightened rabbit. Half-way dismounted; his motions slowed. A timid seven-year-old, he was here to gain confidence, a decision Jamie still debated. Talk of the famous Lady Aalis, the kidnapped French wife of the original owner, wasn't likely to do it.

"Ghosts aren't real." Jamie lied with a conviction as strong as his belief they did. His gaze wandered up the tower. One story claimed they had locked her in for a year before she jumped from the window. Another swore she'd died birthing twins begotten as a result of his ancestor's rape. The stories claimed she'd cursed his great-great-great-grandfather and his children. Whatever the truth, the family's history was riddled with misfortune and the story lost to the bards. What he hid from the group was his hope that if he restored the castle, he might be able to satisfy the ghost and reverse the blight destined to destroy his line.

"Are ye certain?" The trust that lay in Rory's question pushed the doubts aside, and Jamie turned a heart-felt smile on the youngster.

"Aye." Jamie ruffled the mop of red hair. "And even if they are, I'll not let them hurt ye."

Uncertain, Rory clutched the reins of his small piebald and eyed the walls suspiciously. "Do ye think there's hidey-holes in it?"

"I'm sure there are." Jamie chuckled to himself. Had the boy's fascination with tunnels and priest holes always been there, or had the fateful massacre that had taken Rory's mother and his own family created it?

Jamie shoved the thought aside. "Paddy, why don't you and Rory see if you can find a dry room inside while we get the lay of the land?"

Reaching for the lead string, Jamie took Rory's mount and his own and began to tend them. Around him, his men began to do the same, one taking two mounts while others started preparations for the night or explored the ruins. Mentally, Jamie ran through the necessary tasks, pairing them up with the names of the men to make sure they performed them all. There was no need. They were aware of what to do. They'd been doing it their entire lives. Just not for him.

"Do ye hear that?" Jock asked.

The rest stiffened and spun toward him, hands reaching for their weapons. Jock stood in the center of the rubbish-strewn courtyard, face raised toward the sky, with as beatific an expression as Jamie had ever seen.

"All I hear is birds." Malcolm stabbed at a pile of leaves in the corner. A squeal split the air, and a dead squirrel flipped through the air.

"Aye. That's the point. No chatty womenfolk. No babes underfoot. Tis heaven." Jock drew in a lengthy breath, then exhaled. "Even smells quiet."

"Ye just be getting old and crotchety," Malcolm said with a chuckle.

Many of them were here in search of peace and quiet. MacGregor castle had become a noisy, overflowing home after the laird wed. While his new wife was well-loved, her presence had changed things. The long nights spent around the blazing hearth, drinking and telling tales of battles and cattle raids had given way to female chatter and early nights. As always, the clan followed the laird's lead, pairing up in increasing numbers and adding to their families with alarming speed. For some, such as Jamie and Jock, the reminder of what they'd lost became too much. For Malcolm and others, the domestic bliss was too tame.

"I, for one, would rather smell rabbit roasting." A lean, stealthy figure slid from the shadows to toss three rabbits at Jock's feet before crossing to Jamie. The forward scout, Carson Sinclair nodded in greeting then dropped his voice. "There's no one within miles, but an extra guard tonight wouldna be amiss. Someone passed through recently."

He handed a scrap of cloth to Jamie. Too small to tell them much, the coarse, muddy linen displayed jagged edges, as if ripped from a larger cloth.

"Doubtful it's anyone of concern. They trampled the bushes something fierce, so they not be trying to hide, but I lost the trail a short ways back." Carson's brow wrinkled, a sign that worried Jamie more than his words. Carson was able to track a mouse through a briar bush. "It's this God-awful rain, I think. Wiped the hoof prints away."

"Just one?"

"Aye. Someone small. Had I not found that"—he gestured at the cloth with his chin—"I would have thought it was a runaway pony. Found the scrap a mile or two back."

Carson turned away, tossing his plaid back to wring out the excess water, a sign he'd said everything there was to say. That he'd spoke at all caused a shiver of concern. Of the bunch, Carson was the least likely to worry. He didn't fear much of the unknown and even less of the known.

Jamie glanced at the tower and another sliver of premonition sluiced through him. He tried to shake it off, but as he did, the sound of running feet, breaking twigs, and labored breathing broke out.

This time, steel shrieked. Stones rattled and curses arose. Moments later, Rory hurtled through a gap in the bushes, Patrick scrambling on his heels.

"I seen her! I seen her!"

The men closed ranks, backs to one another. Rory skidded to a halt. Patrick tripped, nearly running over him. Everyone glared at the bushes while Rory bent over, gasping for air.

"Twasn't her." Patrick wheezed out and dragged one hand through his copper hair. "But twas something in there." His dirk pointed toward a rock outcropping behind the trees.

"Twas so! She talked to me."

Patrick shook his head. Jamie's grip loosened, but his sword remained poised to strike. A quick glance at Carson conveyed his intentions and sent another two men off into the woods.

"What did she say?" Jamie asked when Rory wiped his hands and straightened. And how had they ended up in the woods outside the castle?

"She said to be careful."

Wordlessly, two more men melted into the darkness encroaching on the courtyard.

"Jock, stay here with Rory." Jamie's fingers tightened around his sword hilt, and he drew a dirk from his boot. Malcolm, Paddy, and Carson followed suit.

"No!" Rory launched himself and wrapped his thin arms around Jamie's forearm. "Please!"

The dirk slipped from Jamie's fingers, clattering against a stone.

"Egads, boy." Careful to avoid the youngster's head, Jamie swung his sword arm to the right and wrapped his left around the boy's waist. The slight figure shook and buried his face in Jamie's stomach.

"Please, Laird. Let me come."

Jamie dropped to his knees. "Ack, Rory boy. Tisn't safe. Ye just said so."

The carrot curls bounced. "Nay. The Lady told me." His face screwed up, and his lip quivered. "I don't want to be left behind." His chin rose in false bravado. "Not again."

Paddy stepped forward and laid a hand on Rory's shoulder. "Stay close to me, brat, or I'll slice the curls off yer head meself." He handed the boy a razor-sharp dirk. "And be careful ye dinna stab me by mistake."

They edged forward, falling into order automatically before he mumbled, "And twasn't Lady Aalis."

Carson led, figure crouched as his gaze leapt from the ground to the bushes and back. Within minutes, they traversed the underbrush and stood before a crack in the mountain. Barely wide enough to fit a man, the fissure hid behind a thicket of burnet roses yet to bloom.

Jock eyed the opening warily. "Guess I'll guard the entrance. Paddy, how d'ye get in from the inside?"

"There's an opening in the kitchen. Looks like a shelf hid it."

"Remind me not to send you and Rory next time something needs exploring," Jamie drawled.

At his gesture, Malcolm snaked back the way they'd come. His friend's muscles and girth were too large to fit through the crack. Reduced to four, one of which might prove more a liability than an asset, Jamie reconsidered his decision. One look at Rory's face prevented a reversal. The boy stared up at him with utter faith, dirk clutched at the ready.

With a sigh, Jamie pulled out a taper and lit it. "Stay back from the light. Let me and Carson be the target." Rory edged closer to Patrick, and Jamie followed Carson through the cleft, squeezing his shoulders through the rock with an oomph.

The short tunnel widened once he eased through. Before him, the whisper of Carson's feet mixed with the sputter of the flame. Jamie slinked forward until the light widened into a small cavern.

"Looks like your ancestors expected trouble," Carson remarked.

Scattered throughout the cavern, rusty weapons lay

in pieces, interspersed with broken barrels and old bones. Jamie kicked at one. Light gleamed off the white bone, a fox skull, accentuating the empty orbs where eyes had been.

"Aye." The taper barely revealed the surrounding area. Shadows multiplied beyond that, but darker pockets suggested other exits. As he stepped toward the center, he glanced back, hand shielding the flame. Sure enough, a faint brightening beckoned from behind Rory and Patrick.

"We were picking through that," Patrick said and pointed his sword at a pile of rotten garments spilling out of a disintegrating trunk, "when we heard it."

"Twas the ghost." Rory's whisper sounded loud, bouncing off the close walls.

Jamie winced and lifted a finger to his lips.

"Go away." The moan slithered up Jamie's spine.

Rory jumped. The light of his taper bounced off the whites of his eyes, darting like a scurrying mouse.

Off to his right, Carson's plaid whispered as he slipped farther into the shadows. Jamie moved left, swinging the light outward in order to leave Rory and Patrick cloaked in darkness.

"Come no closer." Breathy and unreal, the words were more a moan than a command.

"Name yourself." Jamie raised the taper. The light danced, swallowed as quickly as it landed.

A scrape snapped him to the left. A muttered curse filled the air. His jaw tightened.

In Gaelic, he asked, "What were you and Rory talking about in here, Paddy?"

Patrick followed his lead, responding in their native tongue. "Whether Lady Aalis would hurt anyone or not."

"Go!" the voice urged. "Ere it's too late."

The spirit still spoke in English, but the words strengthened Jamie's conviction. Whoever it was, they'd used Rory's fear against him. While they might understand Gaelic, they might not be skilled enough to answer. Lady Aalis had been French, proficient in neither Gaelic nor English.

"If you're Lady Aalis," he said in French, "name your kidnapper."

Another shuffling sound narrowed the location, and the shadow that was Carson eased closer. Jamie waited for the response, jaw clenched, suspecting none.

"Please," the would-be ghost begged, in French. "I don't want to hurt you."

A second later, a scream erupted, deafening and shrill. Jamie lunged forward. Something crashed into him, arms and legs flailing. The taper hurtled to the ground. Carson cursed, and Jamie's shin exploded with pain. When another shape slammed against him, his sword hand smashed into the wall. His weapon clanged against the stone.

With a calculated swipe, Jamie reached out. His fingers latched onto thin bone and locked. He hauled it close, latching an arm about the small frame. Another frightened wail raised hackles on his neck. Tiny hands and feet pummeled him, like a barrage of snowballs thrown by weaklings, constant but harmless. His captive wrenched free. He surged forward. A form collapsed beneath him, bony and wet. A whoosh of air burst in his face, but as he reached out, the figure slipped away. A scrambling noise directed him to the right. With a final burst of speed, he wrapped his arms around a writhing form.

"No!" A wrenching sob tore the air. Tiny hands locked onto his arms, scratching and pushing to no avail. He tightened the embrace, lifting the form from the ground. Feet thrashed at his thighs, one lucky swing connecting with his nutmegs.

He sucked in a breath and held tighter. Terror soaked into him. Frail ribs heaved beneath icy skin; raspy panicked breaths beat at him. The entire form shook.

"Ack, *aon bheag*," he whispered as a curly head banged at his neck and chest. "I'll not hurt ye." Over and over he repeated the assurance while futile blows batted at him. To prove the point, he gentled his grip, holding on just enough to restrain the child. Finally, with gasping sobs of desperation, the figure sagged in his arms.

"Is she all right?" Rory asked, voice trembling. "Lady Aalis says she's hurt."

"I dinna ken." Jamie lifted the limp figure and cradled it in the dark. Lighter than an armful of kindling, with limbs so thin he feared they might snap, she slumped against him. Childish whimpers clutched at his heart while bone-chilling frost sucked the warmth from him. "But she'll freeze to death if we dinna get her warmed up."

Chapter Two

Sarah battled sleep. She ought to be scared. She remembered a vise-like embrace that stole her breath and a searing bolt of pain in her chest. She ought to fight but her limbs refused. She ached all over, but the pain no longer burned. And the bone-rattling chill didn't stab her with every breath she took.

She must be dead.

But that wasn't possible. If she was, Hammond had been wrong.

Or maybe her idea of Hell was inaccurate.

Heat enveloped her, a living, breathing warmth she had never experienced. It beckoned, promising rest if only she allowed it, but a strange music claimed her attention. Hushed lilts swirled through her consciousness, swelling and receding, with bouts of quiet laughter interspersed. As she listened, words crystallized. Gaelic words. Some she'd heard in Mitchell Castle, but here they sounded mellow and pleasing, not guttural and harsh.

Satan must be busy.

She tried to lift her eyelids. Deep melodious words of cleaning and repairing walls reached her, along with discussions of oats and herbs, sheep and cattle, and neighboring clans. Every so often, heat rumbled and a word or two blasted out, then a flash of warmth ran along her arm. Every stroke made it harder to open her eyes.

She sighed and burrowed deeper into the warmth. Hell even smelled good—maple and something else, something musky she didn't recognize. Maybe the maple meant they had food.

Her eyelids drifted open. Red points of light danced before her, too busy for her to focus. The music stopped. The waves of comfort stalled.

Hell, then.

Disappointed, she gave up and let her eyes close.

A growl filled the air, eating at her from the inside out.

Funny, she hadn't expected to be hungry in Hell.

"Have ye come back to us, lass?"

Satan spoke English? Confused, she shook her head. Hell shook, a gentle rolling vibration that shook her bones.

"If ye wake up, we'll feed ye." The trembling died away, and the comforting heat trailed the length of her arm. "Ye had us worried. Twould be a boon if ye'd wake and eat a wee bit."

Something cool touched her lips. The lyrical voice coaxed her to drink. Parched, she forced her lips to part. Moisture dribbled down her throat.

"More," she croaked. Her hands leapt up and fastened on what seemed like molten iron. It rippled, though, and pulled the liquid away.

She forced her eyes open. Numerous red eyes gazed at her. She squeezed hers shut again. She didn't want to be in Hell. Not even a warm, comfortable one. Once, as a little girl, she'd thought it might be a nice place to live. Her uncle, the Devil of the Highlands, was her favorite person at the time. Now, she knew it was just a nickname, given to her uncle by the enemies who hated and feared him. He wasn't an actual devil.

"Tiny sips, *aon bheag*." Metal touched her lips again. She swallowed. The dry burn eased.

Aon bheag. She didn't understand that one. He'd called her that before. When he captured her.

She lifted her eyelids again. Still the eyes watched. But there were smiles, too. When she opened her lips to speak, another soothing wash trickled down her throat.

Perhaps Hell wasn't so bad.

Her eyelids fluttered, too heavy to lift, and she leaned back into the cocoon of warmth, resigned. Fingertips brushed along her temple, then through her hair.

"Am I in Hell?" she croaked, wincing. She sounded like a hag, her voice so scratchy and strange it hurt after their musical tones.

"Ha!" Startled, her eyes flew open. A log bounced, and the fire sparked. "Probably seems like it, waking to this bunch." A giant turned and poked at the flames with another log. Clad in yards of blue and green tartan, he had a barrel chest and arms that rippled with muscle. She'd thought Hammond's men were huge, but this man dwarfed every one of them. Covered in umber hair, he resembled the poor bearskin rug in Hammond's study.

A bear with blue eyes…that spoke English?

"Does Hell have ghosts?" a high pitched voice asked.

"Enough about the ghost, Rory." The words sent ripples through her, tinged as they were with amusement. "Ye'll frighten the Sassenach."

"She's not scared."

Flashes of memory arose as her gaze wandered toward the voice. A skinny boy with hair the color of the exotic oranges her father used to bring home, he shot her a hesitant smile. She'd heard him, and another, talking of a ghost while she cowered in the cave. It had been a good idea, trying to frighten them away. But it hadn't worked.

"I bet Lady Aalis—"

"Enough!" Instantly, the boy clamped his lips shut and sat back, sullen and scowling.

"I'm…not afraid of ghosts." Sorry for the boy, she forced the words out, along with a wary smile. Ghosts were one of the few things that didn't frighten her. She'd grown up alone, with only *imaginary* friends for company. She'd learned to not mention them. The boy would, too.

He peeked at her, and his face relaxed.

Confident now that she didn't reside in Hell, Sarah surveyed her surroundings.

When she'd crawled through the crack, she'd been desperate. She'd walked out of Hammond's keep, garbed in the uniform of a page, then climbed up on the old pony she'd named Romeo. They'd trudged through the mud and rain for hours, hoping her absence would go unnoticed long enough to wash the tracks away. Romeo had been too heavy though, and staying atop him had terrified her, so when she fell, she'd left him. The fall had knocked the breath from her, and burning stabs of pain had plagued her after, but she didn't dare ask for help.

She'd left Romeo near a croft, hoping the residents would give him a better life than Hammond had. For days, she'd rambled through the countryside, sleeping beneath budding bushes for short periods of time before trudging along muddy foot paths and deer trails. When she'd crawled into the last set of briars, she'd been ready to die, as beaten by the Highland cold, hopeless fatigue, and unrelenting hunger as she'd been by Hammond's versions of penance.

The cut in the mountain had opened for her, luring her in with promises of endless sleep. The tiny space terrified her as much as climbing atop Romeo. Dark and cramped, she'd called on her last vestige of courage to crawl into the earth. She wasn't sure how long she slept, but when she'd heard the voices, she thought Hammond had found her.

She still wasn't certain he hadn't.

She counted six around the fire; the boy and the giant, and four others. One looked her age, maybe a few years older, with hair that gleamed like copper in the firelight. She'd never seen one of Hammond's men smile as he did, though. Someone called him Paddy. The others ranged in size and age, from an older, short man puffing on a pipe to the handsome fellow they called Carson, who moved as silently as a tree swaying in the wind. He crossed the space now, bowl in hand, to offer the promised food.

She stared, too weak to turn and face her demon captor, as a hand reached out from behind. Tanned fingers with trimmed nails gripped the wooden bowl. Callouses marred the smooth skin in spots, but they were neither as soft as Euanan's nor as rough as the men who worked for Hammond. His body was hard. A solid shoulder cradled the back of her head, flexing beneath supple muscles as he adjusted their position. Strong thighs lifted her as if she weighed nothing, and the stomach against her back was as tight as Romeo's hide.

Fingers wrapped around the spoon and stirred the mixture. Maple wafted upward, tickling her senses.

Heat flooded her face as an angry growl emanated from her stomach.

A chuckle stirred the curls behind her ear, and the spoon floated toward her. "Not too much. Ye'll want to wolf it down, but it will come back up if ye do."

She didn't care. Her mouth engulfed the spoon. Flavor exploded on her tongue. She closed her eyes, but tears leaked out. When she swallowed, a trapped sob convulsed through her body.

"Ack, *aon bheag*," the voice dripped as sweetly as the maple. He set the bowl aside and hugged her. "You're safe now. We'll not let ye starve. Are ye lost?"

She shook her head, her cheek rubbing against wool as soft as a cloud. Beneath it, his chest was as hard as marble. He was strong enough to kill Hammond. But she didn't want Hammond dead. She just never wanted to lay eyes on him again.

"No." She sniffled and tried to push herself up. The arms locked around her. She fell back, still too weak to fight.

"Who do ye belong to, lass? We'll send word so they can come and get ye."

She shook her head again, panic rising. Fear cramped her stomach, gnawing deeper than the hunger. Her hands clawed at his arms.

"No, please. I can't go back."

The arms tightened. She gasped, certain her lungs were on fire. Instantly, the hold relaxed.

"I canna keep ye here." Worry laced the words.

"Tis no place for a young girl. And we've no one to take care of ye."

"Please." Desperate, she twisted to look at him, but pain exploded in her ribs. Instead, she fell back and clutched the comforting forearm. "I'll behave. I'll do anything you ask." She burrowed into his chest to hide the tears leaking out. "Don't send me back."

****

"Are ye feeling better, lass?"

Unable to resist, Jamie pushed a golden curl back to get a better look at her. As soft as goose down, the short locks trapped his knuckle as surely as the girl had caught his attention. He'd held her and cleaned her up, and now he couldn't banish her from his mind.

Long, matching gold lashes fluttered. A pair of indescribable blue eyes blinked, then widened. As blue as the Highland sky on a cloudless day or Loch Lomond sparkling in the sun, they were eyes that might drown a man. Against the vivid purple and green bruise on her temple, they resembled blue ice.

"Where am I?" Her gaze crawled over the cave, a frown marring her smooth forehead. In the center of the cavern, a fire roared, chasing away the chill and damp that had lined the walls when they arrived. Her thin arms still hugged her chest, then her eyes locked on him. "Who are you?"

"You may call me Jamie." He smiled in an attempt to put her at ease, but her brows lowered further. Surprised, he stepped away. Her gaze followed the way a cornered rabbit watched a hunter. "We found you hiding here," he continued. "Tis a tunnel system behind my castle."

"I...remember." Her gaze floated over their

supplies, taking in the disarray of ten men, but every time it landed on him, it skittered away. "Thank you," she said and glanced down. Her hand hovered over the wool blanket, then caressed it as if it were the finest brocade. A flicker of desire shot through his groin.

"There's no need. I've done naught that any other man would have done." He turned away to hide the lie. Ever since he'd cleaned her up, his cock had been teasing him. Not the child he'd thought, she'd bound her breasts, which had probably been a boon considering her rib was either cracked or broken. When he'd freed them, they'd proven generous and soft, just the way he liked them. Her smooth skin confirmed what her speech suggested. Whoever she was, she was highborn, not some lowborn wench to dally with. Only his prick argued that fact, reminding him it had been months since he'd lain with a woman.

"Still," she said in a voice just as soft, "you've been kind and Poppa always said kindness should be rewarded."

"And your poppa is…"

"Dead."

He whirled. She'd used the past tense. Ordinarily, he would have picked up on it. Instead, he'd made her pale lips tremble.

"I'm sorry." He dragged a hand over the back of his neck and looked away. His usual flair for words was nowhere to be found, lost in the thought of how her lips would taste.

"You didn't know. And it was a while ago. I should be over it by now."

And he shouldn't be mourning Joan either, yet he was. "How long ago was it?"

"Almost three years."

His harrumph echoed, but he left it at that.

If she had no father, then she'd fled someone else. A husband? The idea made him scowl. "Can ye tell me your name?"

"No."

When his head snapped around, her chin rose. But she still avoided his gaze.

"Why not?"

"It's not important."

Something told him that was a lie. The way she twirled her finger in her hair, perhaps. Not that he blamed her. Her hair was as soft as the last note of a lament. It had tickled his neck the entire night.

Focus, MacIan. Ye're not here to tup her. Ye're here to figure out who she is.

"Tis important to me," he said.

"Why?"

Jamie rolled his eyes and circled the cave. She'd slept for three days. Three days that had left him a man short, plus Gus, who had gone back to MacGregor castle for reinforcements and information. He needed those two men but leaving her here in the cave alone wasn't feasible. He'd never again leave a woman unprotected.

"I canna keep ye here, lass. I would if I could, but I canna."

The shudder as she inhaled climbed up his back, weighing on him as if the cave walls had collapsed.

"I understand." Her tone said otherwise, and when he turned back, one hand strangled the blanket and the other tugged at her hair. When her eyes lifted, the pleading expression ripped at his loins. "I'll leave as soon as I'm able."

"And go where?"

She shrugged. The blanket slipped and a curve of breast peeked out.

The ache in his groin intensified.

"Just tell me your name. Surely, there's someone who'll take care of you."

"There's no one."

"Everyone has someone." Except that wasn't true. He had Rory and Jock, but if they'd died all those years ago, he'd have had no one. Bryan had taken them in, but only after months traveling from clan to clan. They'd have starved if his voice hadn't been so well known and sought after.

She was still playing with her hair though.

"Can ye at least tell me your first name? Or shall I continue to call ye lass?"

The hint of a smile eased over her lips, and her hand dropped. "Sarah."

"There, now, see? That dinna hurt, did it?"

"No." A shy wash of color pinkened her cheeks, and her gaze skipped away as soon as his locked on hers.

More in line with the usual reaction he received from women, Jamie relaxed. He was getting somewhere. If he turned on his usual charm, she'd tell him anything he asked.

"I imagine you're a tad hungry." He crossed the space and rummaged through a leather satchel. A wrinkled apple appeared, and a bit of dried kipper. He palmed them and grabbed a flask of water, then returned. With a careful squat designed to hide the bulge of his errant cock, he placed the apple in her hand. His fingers lingered, brushing hers before holding out the kipper and flask with his other hand.

Her smooth brow furrowed. Her fingers trembled, and she swallowed. "But it's not mealtime."

He cocked his head. Her mouth watered. Her eyes never left the food. "Did they starve ye, Sarah?"

"No." Her head swiveled, curls bouncing back firelight, but her eyes devoured the apple.

She believed it, that they hadn't. Anger swirled in his gut. Despite her soft round breasts and ample hips, his two hands were able to circle her tiny waist and still leave a void. Her ribs showed, and the only accurate description for the hollows in her face was gaunt.

Still, she was pretty. She'd be gorgeous when healthy.

He lifted her hand and curled his fingers over hers and the apple.

"Here, we eat when we're hungry." He forced himself to smile. "Or at least until it's all gone."

Her grip tightened on the meager fruit, so he released his hold. She swallowed again, then dragged her gaze away, turning it on him. The kiss of her eyes crippled him. She looked at him as if he were the archangel Raphael, the angel of healing.

And all he wanted to do was kiss her.

He bounded to his feet.

"Eat, Sarah. We'll talk later."

After he dealt with his rebellious cock and the equally annoying urge to promise protection.

****

After an entire day lugging stones and hewing trees to repair the wall and gate, Jamie's muscles burned. It did nothing to scorch away the worry that weighed on him.

After downing half a pail of water, then dumping the rest over his sweaty chest, he dropped to the newest felled oak and struggled to catch his breath.

"We dinna need the gate up tomorrow, ye ken?"

Jamie shot a scowl at Malcolm. "Are ye sure?" He gestured at Sarah, reclining on a plaid across the courtyard. His eyes lingered. Too pale and too thin, he reminded himself it had only been three days. The bruises were fading, and she was able to move without wincing. She'd even begun to smile. Not at him, but at most of them. Right now, her face beamed like warm sunshine while Rory chattered beside her, sharpening axes. The irritation multiplied. "What if they come looking for her? We've only nine men."

Malcolm's grin split his face. "Nine o' us against most men? I think the odds are on our side."

"Mayhap. But we don't ken who it is or how many will come." Or why.

"We'll ken soon enough, I expect." Malcolm pulled a flask from his sporran and drank deeply. "Someone like that doesn't just vanish without anyone looking for her. She's a lady. And she's pretty."

The pronouncement tightened Jamie's jaw. "Aye, she's pretty." Why did he care that Malcolm thought so or that she smiled at everyone but him?

He dragged himself to his feet and attacked the tree, slamming wedges into a large crack; one every few inches. He'd pounded them the entire length before realizing that Malcolm wasn't helping.

He turned to find his friend studying him, head cocked to one side.

"That what's bothering ye?" Malcolm asked. "That

she's pretty?"

"No." Jamie swiped at the sweat dripping over his cheek, knowing he lied. He'd always had a penchant for dainty women. Joan had been tiny, too. "It's her stubbornness that bothers me."

She refused to tell them where she came from or who she was, aside from her given name. And every time he asked, the fear crept back into her eyes, clouding the watery blue depths, followed by some ludicrous declaration that she'd leave as soon as she was able.

She'd have to cripple him before he'd let her.

"It might help if ye stopped glaring at her."

"I don't glare at her!"

"Aye, ye do. When ye aren't staring at her as if she's a toffee pudding."

Did he stare? He rotated his shoulders while he considered it. "I don't like toffee pudding."

Malcolm started to chuckle, then threw his head back and roared. With a shake of his head, he grabbed his hammer. It swung in a wide arc, and the tree shuddered. A second blow set up a screeching groan before a massive girth split the entire length.

Why had he bothered with the wedges?

"Have Paddy talk to her. She likes him, and he's good at prying out information." Malcolm set the hammer aside, and Jamie scowled. The man didn't even sweat. His own shirt stuck like wet mud, but nothing but a faint sheen showed on his friend. At times like this, he hated Malcolm. The smithy didn't doubt their ability to protect her. And neither did any of the other men.

What would happen when they realized the truth?

He couldn't protect her, and he couldn't protect them. Not with only nine or ten men. Why had he ever concocted this scatterbrained idea?

A second later, Malcolm threw his arm around Jamie's shoulder and pushed the flask at him. "Dinna worry. She'll come around."

"Aye," he lied. Fact was, it didn't matter if she trusted him. And it didn't matter that she avoided him as if he were a poisonous spider.

All that mattered was keeping everyone safe.

Chapter Three

Euanan glared at the troop of men who'd gone after the chit. Mud caked their boots, and untrimmed, scraggly beards hid their faces. Like all his father's men, they were incompetent slobs not worth the steel they wielded.

"What do you mean you can't find her?" His hand slapped the desk, and he rose. "She's a useless cripple with the intelligence of a gnat. How far could she have gone, dragging her ugly leg behind her?"

"By the time we ken she was gone, the tracks was gone," the leader whined, eyeing Hammond in the corner while he cowered before Euanan, head bowed. Behind him, four of their best scouts clumped in the shadows, avoiding eye contact with either man. "Only way we tracked her was because of the pony."

The scouts were as inept as the guards. Blind idiots, the sentries never saw her leave. Who knows how long she'd been gone? That she'd duped the maid with her pile of rags on the bed didn't surprise him, but the guards earned good money to keep an eye on who came and went through the gates.

"I told ye she was devil born," his father said from the corner.

Rage flashed through Euanan. This whole mess was Hammond's fault. She'd have been perfectly amenable to marrying him, if not for the beatings. Now she'd escaped. Her wealth and influence were trickling from his fingers as steadily as hourglass sand. Every minute she evaded him meant another minute for Alexander Campbell to return from France. The wedding needed to happen before that. Her uncle would have no choice but to accept the marriage once her maidenhead broke.

"Get back out there," he hissed, his father's misgiving echoing in his head. She'd not cowered enough at the last beating to stir Hammond's lust. If they didn't find her soon, he'd have to do the deed himself. "I want every able-bodied man out looking. I want the countryside scoured. Every croft, every castle, every copse of trees gets searched until you find her."

****

"I don't think he likes me."

Sarah stared across the room and hugged the pile of blankets she carried, not realizing she'd spoken aloud until Jock snorted.

"Jamie?" he asked, one gray brow lifting before his gaze skidded across to join hers.

On the far side of the room, Jamie and Malcolm piled firewood into an alcove, arms rippling with each toss. The contrast was striking. Beside Malcolm, Jamie looked small, despite a mere two-inch difference in height. With a trim frame and dirty blond locks, he reminded her of an Adonis sculpted by Corradini or Soldani-Benzi, whereas Malcolm made her think of the Norse god Odin.

"He likes ye." Jock turned back to situate the chair he'd been lugging. Utilitarian and plain, the chair nonetheless amazed Sarah. Two days ago, they'd had no furniture, just boxes and logs to sit on, and now an entire dining set had materialized beneath Jock's tools. She'd never have thought to fashion a table from a plank and square bits of wood, let alone put together one so fine. "If he didn't, he'd have tupped ye by now."

Jamie's head shot around. He cleared his throat and glared at the older man. Jock turned as scarlet as a rowan berry.

She'd heard the word before when Hammond's men talked about her and her crippled leg, but she didn't know what it meant, just that her leg wouldn't stop them. Ever curious, she debated asking, but Jock's mumbled apology convinced her otherwise.

"Where should I put these?" She nodded at the pile of blue and green tartan wool she clutched.

This morning, Jamie had declared they would move into the castle proper, and they'd been cleaning out this room and another to accomplish it. Still weak and sore, Sarah's efforts had been minimal, but still her muscles burned, and her leg protested from overuse.

"Over here," Jamie barked and pointed at the second alcove on the opposite side of the fireplace.

Sarah swallowed and dropped her gaze, painfully aware of his. Jock might claim he liked her, but Jamie MacIan's actions said otherwise. Aside from a few gentle words that first day, he'd done nothing but scowl, glower, and bark at her. He watched her every move, as if afraid she'd steal from them.

Bracing herself for the pain, she limped across the room. Larger than Hammond's great room, the distance wasn't huge, but after being on her feet most of the day, it might as well have been miles. Every step jarred, spiking up her leg. A tiny whimper escaped, but amidst the clatter of furniture and men grunting, she doubted anyone heard.

"Dammit, Sarah." Like a swooping hawk, a pair of arms scooped her off the floor. Hazel eyes sparked, green with anger beneath lowering brows. "Why did ye not say ye were hurting?"

God, he's beautiful.

"It's not that bad." She'd suffered worse. It was nowhere near as painful as the first year she broke it. That had been agony. And it didn't compare to the broken rib Hammond had given her.

"Bad or not, from now on, ye will stop when it hurts." In two strides, he crossed to where she'd started and plunked her into the chair Jock had set down. Her eyes widened when he lifted both her and the chair and carried them across the room as easily as a pile of kindling.

"Jock, get me some of that ointment ye use on your shoulder," he ordered before he lifted all but one of the plaids from her arms.

"It's almost gone."

The scowl he shot at Jock scared her, but the older man shrugged and handed him a small jar. Jamie shook out the last plaid and tucked it about her.

"I'm sorry," she said, her voice as meek as possible.

"For what?"

"For being a bother." His hands slowed, and he dropped to his knees. A shiver ran through her. Was this why Poppa had never let a man near her? Because she would want him to hold her?

"Ye arena' a bother, lass. Ye mustn't think that." He hesitated, and Sarah lifted her gaze. He no longer frowned; the wrinkled brow replaced by an unreadable look. It almost felt like a caress the way his gaze drifted over her face.

If only she hadn't had to cut her hair. Instinctively, her hand reached for the shorn locks and heat flooded her face. "I know I'm not beautiful. Not like Momma was. And I know you'd rather I wasn't here." He'd made that plain with his insistent questions about her origins. "But I won't stay long. I won't be any work, and I promise I'll leave as soon as I can."

In response, his head fell forward. A yearning lodged in her throat, and her fingers itched to stroke the dusky gold locks.

His sigh tickled through the thick wool. and she had to squeeze her legs together to quell the strange ache it created.

"Tisn't you who should be sorry, lass." His hand stroked a curl near her ear. "You're no bother, and I've not met a lass as pretty in a good long time. I'm just afraid for you. Afraid I'll not be able to keep you safe. And I dinna like it. But I shouldna take it out on you. I'm sorry."

She offered a weak smile, sure he lied. Poppa had always said handsome men lied, and he was as handsome as they came. But she'd pretend if it meant she didn't have to leave.

"Now, do ye trust me, Sarah?"

She nodded, curious, and a second later, his dirk flashed in his hand. The fingers of his left hand disappeared under the plaid, and she yelped. The bare skin of her left leg convulsed as his hand grasped her calf. Moments later, metal ran up the length of her leg, slicing her stolen breeches from shin to mid-thigh. She stiffened until his hands reappeared, and the green glass jar materialized.

The grin he flashed melted her insides.

A pungent smell wafted up as he rubbed his fingers into the jar. Camphor and a hint of rosemary faded into the smell of a forest.

"The MacGregor's healer makes this. Tis said to be a miracle oil." The smell permeated the air as he rubbed it over his hands, then he reached back under the plaid and gently grasped her knee.

Instinctively, she tensed.

"Relax, *aon bheag*," he said, and his fingers began to knead the muscles behind her knee.

She swallowed as tingles ran up and down her legs. Even her stomach quivered.

"What's that mean?" she asked, grasping onto anything that would keep her focus on something other than his hands.

"*Aon bheag*? It means little one."

She frowned. His grin widened, stealing her irritation.

"*Mo neach beag gaisgeil.* My brave little one. Do you like that better?"

How could she not? Especially when the harsh lines of his face vanished, leaving behind the visage of the boy he must have been, carefree and joyous.

Gentle fingers dug into the muscle atop her thigh, pressing the tension out and away, and she groaned. It was wonderful. If she died this instant, she'd have no regrets.

His thumb and fingers ran along her calf, circling her kneecap, then over the lower portion of thigh, massaging the tightness of the muscles in a slow, rhythmic pattern. Each pass sucked the tension from the rest of her body until she found herself slumping in the chair.

"Does it help, lass?"

"It's wonderful." Heat sank through the skin, easing into her core. Her bones were molten, too soft to hold her. Even the ever-present knot of pain loosened.

"I'm glad." He continued rubbing the fragrant ointment into her skin. "And ye'll stay here as long as ye need."

****

Could she stay forever?

She took another bite of the trout Carson had caught. Flavored with mushrooms and roots, the succulent flesh melted on her tongue. She'd thought she'd died and gone to heaven when she tasted the first serving. When Carson decreed the extra should go to their guest, she'd tried to decline, but an angry scowl had darkened Jamie's face until she accepted.

Now, the men sat around the homemade table, tankards of ale replaced by tins of what they called *uisge-beatha,* laughing and reminiscing. Their loud voices competed with each other, creating a din that hurt her ears, and she winced every time Malcolm's palm collided with Jamie's back, hurtling him toward the table, but Jamie merely punched him back and reminded the giant of some other mistake he'd made years ago. Even Rory joined in, his voice hurtling through the air as he climbed on his chair and demonstrated a move he'd seen one of the men make.

They argued and pounded on each other and—for the moment at least—totally forgot she existed. She sat at a safe distance, soaking up the blazing heat of the fire, and savored the experience. Only Jock noticed her, flashing her a smile from the far end of the table.

"Enough," the elder man bellowed, slamming his tin on the table over and over until the din faded. "Tisn't a proper celebration," he announced when they turned toward him, "until our new laird lifts his voice."

"What would ye have me sing, old man?" Jamie asked.

"Ye ken my favorite." Everyone stilled, and the last vestiges of merriment fell away. "But it shall be the last time we hear it, and ye must follow it with something less melancholy." Jock's hand shook as he reached for the bottle of whiskey and poured a generous splash into each cup. He gestured to Paddy. "Give the lass a cup, too, lad."

"Are ye sure, Jock?" Jamie's voice held a heaviness Sarah had never heard, and the scraping of his chair broke what had become a heavy silence. His figure loomed over the table, face glowing in the flickering light, but a shadow lay over his features.

"Aye, lad. We've mourned long enough. Tis time we put it behind us." The silver of Jock's eyes sparked as he glanced at her, drawing Jamie's greenish hazel gaze with it. Their eyes connected, and Sarah's throat constricted.

No one spoke. All she heard was the soft crackling of the fire and the trickle of whiskey filling one final cup.

Finally, with a single nod, Jamie pushed his chair back. Paddy passed her a cup while the other men lifted the table away to leave a space before the fireplace. Rory's coltish limbs bounded across the space to grab a fiddle off the mantle as everyone settled themselves in a semi-circle.

Hesitantly, Jamie plucked the taut strings, tightening one or two with a pained expression. Then he met Jock's gaze once more and lifted his cup.

Jock stood and cleared his throat. Light glistened around his eyes, and he raised his own drink. "Here's to the MacGorans and all our other departed loved ones. May they rest beneath the beloved Highlands and watch over us, knowing we will never forget them." A single tear trickled the ridge of his cheek, disappearing into the pewter beard as he touched the cup to his lips.

In unison, they muttered in agreement, then threw back the contents of their cups.

Tears burned Sarah's eyes, as much from the searing burn racing down her throat as from the sentiment. Then the most mournful, mellow sound she'd ever heard filled the room.

It wasn't music. She'd heard music, even played it herself. This was more than music.

It started off airy and light, like butterflies dancing across her heart. It trilled up her core, a vibration that made it impossible not to smile. Then the joy multiplied, the tempo gradually increasing until she imagined the stars swirling in the sky. Within the notes, a voice crept in, soft and breathy, as sweet as any woman's.

Mesmerized, Sarah stared. Jamie's head fell back, throat rippling, eyes closed, while his fingers coaxed the melody from the instrument and the song from his heart.

No one else moved, nor made a single sound. Reverent and soul-wrenching, the tune swelled, wrapping in on itself to turn dark and passionate. Before her eyes, the image of swords slashed and flames licked the air. Her lungs scorched, and pain stabbed through her. The words meant nothing to her. In Gaelic, they might as well have been Greek, but the tone articulated the violence and sorrow. The bow flew across the strings, screeching and pounding, while his voice boomed with thunder.

Through it all, tears streamed down his face, slipping from his clean-shaven chin like the stars that had swirled in the sky when he started.

Then, suddenly, it died, replaced by a mournful longing that faded into silence.

Stunned, Sarah couldn't pull her gaze away. Jamie's chest rose and fell, sucking in huge lungs-full of air, and his arms hung at his sides. He looked broken, his body limp and useless.

When Jock clapped him on the shoulder, Jaime's eyes collided with hers, then slid away. He rose, said a word or two to Jock, then slipped from the room. All the warmth left with him.

Carson picked up the fiddle and began to play, a light, simple tune that in comparison reminded her of the lowing of a cow.

Paddy took a seat beside her and refilled her cup. "So, what think ye of MacGoran's Lament?"

"I… It's…" She gave up. She didn't have the words to express it.

"Aye." He nodded sagely, sipping at the fiery liquid. "Tis a fitting requiem. A sad tale it was the first time we heard it, but Jamie's made sure twill ne'er be forgotten."

"What's it about?"

His gaze turned inward before replying. "Tis about Jock and Jamie's clan. And Rory's. Someone slaughtered the MacGorans one night. Nearly two hundred men, women, and children. No one knows who did it, only that no one survived 'cept the three of them. Rory was but a babe. His mum stuffed him in a woodpile." His gaze lingered on Rory, then slid toward the door. "Jock's wife and five children died; his one daughter pregnant with her first child. Jamie's wife had just delivered a little boy the month before. It was the first time he'd left them."

"That's awful!" The whiskey burned and threatened to come back up. How had they survived it?

"Aye. Tis worse that Jamie thinks himself responsible. He kens he couldna have stopped it. But still." He shrugged, a movement that sent his copper hair slipping over his eyes. He pushed it back, a smile peeking out. "Twas a boon for my brother though. He took them in and gained the best bard in all of Scotland. Jamie had been planning on joining the Campbell Clan as their bard but changed his mind. He believed them responsible."

Sarah stiffened. Her mother had been a Campbell.

"What about you, lass? A pretty young thing like yourself must have someone who misses you."

"No. There's no one."

"No? No brothers or sisters? No parents?"

"No." She hugged herself. "No one but me." Was he trying to trick her? Get her to tell him who she was?

What did it matter? Perhaps if she told him a little, they'd stop pestering her.

"Poppa died a few years ago. Momma died last year." She didn't add that since then her life had been hell; a hell punctuated by the fact that she'd been a pampered, spoiled princess before coming to Scotland.

"I'm sorry. I can't imagine how lonely that must be." The pity on his face rankled, so she studied the fire instead.

"It wasn't so bad. I had plenty of servants, and Poppa showered me with gifts and attention." She straightened her back as her uncle had taught her, skipping the fact that Poppa had left her alone most of the time, with a mother who had needed as much care as her daughter and a nursemaid who resented not being in Scotland.

"How about suitors? You must have had one or two."

"No." She clamped her lips closed. She wasn't pretty.

"They must be blind then."

It was too much. Fed up, she jumped to her feet. The plaid slipped to the floor and chill air blasted her leg. Her face heated. She'd forgotten the slit Jamie had created in her breeches, and now they all stared at her crippled leg.

They pretended not to, but she saw it. Just like Hammond's men, they pretended not to look at her. And just like her uncle, they didn't want her. She wasn't pretty. She didn't sing or play a musical instrument like Jamie did, and no one would ever write a song for her. She wasn't strong or smart. She was nothing, nothing but a burden, a crippled, useless burden.

Chapter Four

Jaime lay on his plaid, bone-weary, and watched the firelight dance along the walls. He'd hoped to be further along in their endeavors, but everything proved harder than anticipated. Niall and Logan had arrived two days late with the carts, acceptable oak had been further from the castle than he'd hoped, the well had been so filled with debris, it had taken half a day to dig it out, and his focus was sloppy because of weariness. At this rate, they'd starve or freeze to death this winter.

Behind him, he heard Sarah flip over again. He'd tucked her into the small room off the kitchen, for privacy, while the men bedded down before the fire. The scent of dried apples and spices drifted out, sprinkling him where he guarded the threshold.

What the hell had Patrick said?

Like everything else, the idea to have Patrick try to learn more about her had been ill-advised. Instead of gaining any useful information, all it accomplished was to send her back into her shell.

No parents. No siblings. No suitors. Lots of gifts and servants. No wonder she rarely talked.

Another rustle caught his attention. Was that a sob? No. Just another restless sigh.

He pulled his tartan closer around his shoulders. The air had a bite the cave hadn't. Maybe he shouldn't have rushed the move.

A leak near the wood pile plunked another drop of water. He waited, tense until it splashed. Another task to add to the list. Again, Sarah moved.

Why couldn't he shut her out as completely as she ignored him?

Frustrated, he threw himself over to stare at the ceiling. Rotted beams sagged. Water glistened on the blackened wood before splashing to the floor.

He groaned and threw his hand over his eyes.

He'd thought it would be easier in the castle. Easier to ignore the thrum of desire that trickled up every time he looked at her. Easier to sleep if her delectable ass weren't rubbing areas it oughtn't. Instead, it just felt lonely. And every sound she made left him tense and worried.

A blast of wind sent the fire into a frenzy of activity. Sparks shot into the darkness.

He'd moved them because of his lack of control. Just as he'd dragged them here because he wanted to build something of his own, fuck the consequences. And he'd banished her to the same loneliness she'd lived with her entire life.

A whimper rose up, muffled by the sound of Sarah tossing once more.

"Are ye going to let her freeze to death?" Malcolm grumbled. Wool rustled, and he, too, thudded as his back hit the floor.

"I've fed the fire three times." And stared at the tiny figure as often. The memory of his fingers on her thigh that afternoon still sent shocks of desire through him.

"Aye, well the noise is keeping me awake." A number of mutters emanated from other piles of tartan.

"If ye dinna go and warm her up, I'll do it meself."

Jamie found himself on his feet before the thought even registered. Behind him, Malcolm chuckled. Two steps later, Jamie slipped to the floor and pulled the shivering form against him. His cock applauded, eagerly pushing against the scratchy wool between them.

"Go away."

"Nay." He stroked her arm. Her thin linen shift did little to disguise the iciness of her skin. "Ye're freezing, lass."

"I'm not."

God, she was stubborn.

"Well, something's bothering ye. Ye've been tossing and turning the last two hours. And the chattering of your teeth has Malcolm threatening to toss you out into the rain."

To his shock, she shattered, convulsing with strangled sobs. Tears began to gush, splashing on his arm.

"Ah, *aon bheag,* dinna cry." He wrapped himself around her. Her chill crept over him, but did little to discourage his prick, so he focused on the sound of her sobs. Not knowing the cause, he had no clue how to stop them. And no motivation. He liked that she clung to him, her soft hands clutching his forearm, her cheek rubbing against the hairs.

How selfish was that? How reprehensible that he let his hands roam over her, knowing she was little more than a child.

"You should let him." With a muffled choke, she wiped angrily at her eyes and sniffled.

Jamie's head snapped back, confused. "What?"

"Toss me out. I've no right to be here."

Their earlier conversations replayed, word for word, through his mind, as did the recounting Patrick had given of his aborted effort to learn her lineage. Something had hit a nerve, but what?

"How old are ye, *ao*—" He bit off the endearment. "Sarah?"

"Nineteen." She stiffened then sniffled between bouts of teeth clacking. "Why?"

The air rushed from his lungs. Nineteen? He'd have guessed no more than fifteen. No wonder she objected to *little one*. People probably treated her as a child because of her size. He had.

He replayed what Patrick had told him, wishing Patrick had the same word for word recall he had. Nineteen, and no suitors? Was that what bothered her?

No. Patrick said she stopped talking when he told her Bryan had taken them in.

I'm sorry for being a bother. I know you'd rather I wasn't here. I'll behave. I'll do anything you ask. Toss me out.

His stomach twisted, things she'd said to him echoing in his head as relentlessly as the tasks he hadn't finished.

No siblings. No suitors. Lots of gifts and servants.

But no love. No sense of belonging or acceptance.

Unbidden, his hand slipped over the curve of her hip. Instead of comforting her, it just made his cock twitch again.

"How old were you when you broke your leg?" he asked, concentrating on proper English pronouns as much to distract himself as to make her comfortable.

She hesitated. "Six. I fell off my pony. Poppa was

very angry." Her leg flexed. The movement sent another flash of lust to his groin. "Eilidh said I deserved it, for disobeying."

"Who was Eilidh?"

"My nurse. Well, Momma's actually."

When she snuggled closer and sighed, her ass rubbed against him and his cock swelled.

Focus. She's talking to ye. Don't ruin it with yer randy lack of control.

Jamie threw the plaid off his shoulder and adjusted his position. Sarah wiggled. A hiss split the air, and he slammed a hand on her hip.

"Dinna do that, lass."

"Do what?"

"Squirm."

She stiffened in his arms and stopped talking. Regret welled. He enjoyed her soft curves pressing against him, her whispers in the darkness about things she didn't dare say in the daylight. He eased closer, careful to keep a space between his probing cock and her ass.

"Patrick said ye—you—lost your parents. Do you miss them?"

The answer took so long he feared it wasn't coming. "I miss Poppa." Longing soaked through her, robbing her body of the tension. "He spoiled me. I know that now."

Spoiled? She'd asked for nothing since they found her. If he wasn't so obsessed with her and the problems her presence created, he might forget she existed.

"But not your mother?"

Her head shook, the curls tickling his arm. "Momma was different. She…" He felt her frown.

"Momma wasn't very smart. Poppa told me to take care of her, but I failed."

She shrank in his arms, curling into a ball. Tiny shivers filled the air. Jamie waited, afraid if he said more, she'd pull away again. When she did speak, he had to lean to make out her words.

"I told her not to marry him. But Eilidh liked him. Then he killed her."

"Who? Eilidh or your mother?"

"Momma."

"Who killed her?"

Her head shook harder, so he let it go. In time, she'd tell him.

"It's not your fault, Sarah. You couldn't have stopped it." He laid a comforting hand on her shoulder. She didn't withdraw, so he nestled closer, despite the throb it created. "And I won't let him find you."

She hugged his arm in response. This time, when the silence fell, he let it. It was a comfortable silence. They lay together, and her breathing lengthened. Now and then, she shifted, reaching to rub at her leg or change its position. He ignored the twitching in his cock and focused on the soft sound of her breath, and the sweet smell of apples that lingered in the air. After a time, her body relaxed and snuggled closer.

Talk about sweet torture. Every wiggle sent a burst of lust through him. But her body sinking into him was heaven, as soft and welcome as a summer breeze. He began to count her breaths to distract himself.

She squirmed again. His prick jumped.

The plaid rustled. A hand brushed his stomach.

His abdomen convulsed, robbing his voice of strength. "Don't." Gasping, he clamped his finger around her wrist.

"But there's something hard back there."

His exhale released a tension he'd not acknowledged. They'd not abused her in *that* way. And she wasn't wedded. If she were, she'd know what was poking at her.

"Tis nothing. Just ignore it." He forced the air in and out of his lungs. "I'll take care of it." As extra protection, he tangled his fingers in hers while a trickle of sweat tickled his neck.

"Does it hurt?" she asked moments later, voice hushed and hesitant.

"Does what hurt?" His cock was screaming, but how could she know that?

"Your affliction?"

His head jerked back. "My affliction?"

"I'm sorry. I shouldn't have said anything. It isn't polite." She snatched her hand away and shimmied forward.

He stared at the back of her head. Gold curls winked at him, reddish in the firelight.

"You needn't be embarrassed," she pronounced, flipping onto her back and staring at the ceiling. Her lashes flickered like gossamer wings. "I don't mind. Everyone has things wrong with them. I'm just curious. Ham—" She bit off whatever she'd been about to say. "My stepfather was deformed, too. It would get worse when he was mad. Sometimes, I thought it would burst. I even wanted it to at times." Her face scrunched, eyes clamped shut, jaw tight. "I even hoped it would hurt." When her eyes opened, shame blazed through the dim light, and the knot in his gut tightened. "It won't burst, will it? Because I wouldn't want you to die."

The lust drained away, crowded out by astonishment. She might have been raped. Would have been if she'd not left. But she felt guilty? Because she'd hoped it hurt her stepfather?

"No, *mo neach beag gaisgeil.* Twill not burst."

Not the way she thought at least.

****

"Will ye have another scone, *Aingeal?"*

A hot blush filled Sarah's face as she snapped her gaze toward Jock. One of his silver eyes winked, and a knowing smile split his face.

Sarah dropped her gaze. "No, thank you."

Aingeal. She wasn't an angel. Far from it. Angels didn't stare. And they certainly didn't wonder about being kissed. Which was all she'd been thinking about since last night. It was wicked, resulting as it did from the knowledge that Jamie was as flawed as she.

"Ye'll hurt my feelings if ye dinna." Scarred, rough fingers gently uncurled hers and pressed the warm biscuit into her palm. "And even Rory has had enough to fill his endless gut. Twill just go to waste."

"Very well."

Rory did seem content, with crumbs clinging to his lips. At first, he'd held back around her, wary-eyed and silent, but since Jamie had regulated him to *protecting* her when the men were busy, his curiosity and boyish chatter emerged. The only time he remained quiet was when his stomach was full, as it was now. The youngster grinned at her as he mended one of the ropes.

"Stop flirting with the lass, Jock."

Sarah's head spun around. Jamie's tartan swirled around his knees as he crossed the room, a homespun shirt straining at the shoulders. When he smiled, her

49

mouth went dry and her stomach flipped.

She stuffed the scone between her lips and dragged her gaze away. Previously moist and delicious, it now choked like sand.

"Ye'll stay with the lass, Rory," Jamie continued. "Malcolm and I will be in the west forest. Jock, can ye help Logan repair that leak in the kitchen?"

"Aww," Rory interrupted. "I wanted to help Logan. I never get to do anything important."

"I can stay with our *aingeal*." Jock ruffled Rory's head, earning a scowl. "Let the boy have some fun. I'm gettin' too old to be climbing on roofs, anyway."

Jamie scoffed, but instead of the usual bark that accompanied any question of his orders, he shrugged. "Tis up to Jock. But nothing's as important as watching our *aingeal*, Rory."

Aware of his scrutiny, Sarah looked away, afraid her face would burst into flames if she returned his regard. Somehow, knowing he wasn't as perfect as she'd thought, that he too had a condition he hid, changed things.

"And what about you, Sarah? What will you do today?"

Her head shook, reminding her she'd sacrificed her best feature to aid in her escape.

"Could I ask a favor?" His hair fell forward, accentuating the green in his eyes, a green that seemed brighter today. "Can ye sew?"

"Yes." Her voice squeaked, the scone still stuck in her windpipe, further embarrassing her.

"Could you mend this shirt? I ripped it yesterday."

Stupidly, she just stared, even though he held it out, until one brow rose, and his lips twitched.

He's laughing at you, you dolt.

Her hand shot out and grabbed the shirt.

He's just a man. You've met them before.

She'd never met one who made her lungs stutter when he was around, though, like the air was too thin. Her stomach quivered when he came near. She wanted to cry when he barked at her, and today, when he finally seemed happy, it was like a perfect summer day, warm and bright.

With a hard swallow, she pushed the odd sensations aside.

"Of course." Somehow, the words came out despite the somersaults in her stomach. Rather than look at him, she stretched the shirt out. Her arms hardly extended far enough. "I'm excellent at sewing." A large tear gaped at the shoulder, the edges ragged and torn, but the even weave implied a quality she hadn't expected. "I'll just need some thread and a needle."

"I hate sewing." Rory jumped up and bounded toward a box against the wall. "Tis wimmen's work." He skipped back, a small wooden box in hand. "They always stick me with it."

Jamie cuffed him on the ear, but a glint in his eye betrayed a lack of malice. "In case ye've not noticed, imp, we brought no women with us. And I told you, we all carry part of the load. That's your part."

"But we got her now."

"Sarah's a guest."

Rory's face fell.

Sarah's spine stiffened, and she raised her chin. Any resentment disintegrated at the sly wink Jamie directed toward her. "But twould be a great help."

He pulled the tail of his shirt out to expose a

jagged, unkempt repair. Barely held together, the rip looked like three pairs of puckered lips. He added another comment, something about Rory's stitches, but Sarah couldn't tear her gaze away. Hard, rippling skin peeked beneath the hem. Golden and alive, her fingers itched to reach out and touch it. Instead, she clutched the smooth linen he'd given her.

"Lass?" He snapped his fingers. "Sarah?"

On fire, her face lifted. His eyes blazed back at her, an amused twitch playing over his lips.

God, he was gorgeous. Why had her uncle chosen Euanan and not him?

Like a blast of winter air, the idea slapped her back to reality. Jamie MacIan was the most handsome man she'd ever met. But he didn't look at her with pity or as if he was counting her money as her father had warned her was the only thing handsome men would want from her. All he wanted was a shirt sewn.

"Yes." She hadn't been listening. "Of course, I'll fix it. I'll do anything you need."

Or want.

Glancing around, the truth of her situation stared back. They accepted her just as she was. There was no pity in Carson's eyes. Rory talked a mile a minute to her, the same as he did with everyone, and Jock mothered her in the same manner he did Rory. Niall ignored her, but he largely ignored everyone, and Ramsay grumbled *to* her but never *about* her.

None of them treated her as a useless cripple. They weren't aware she had one of the largest fortunes in England or that she was the niece of a Campbell, one of Scotland's most powerful families. They had no clue about the history that shadowed her life. As handsome as Jamie MacIan might be, to him, she was just a lost girl. And he still smiled at her.

"Is there anything else you'd like me to do?"

Chapter Five

The last oak crashed to the ground the next day,
and Jamie shrugged off the strain of the past two weeks.
They'd cut enough oak to finish the gate and repair the
first-floor beams and struts, the walls were coming
along, and Logan and Ramsay had done wonders
digging up long ago planted potatoes, onions, and
carrots. Barring any unforeseen losses to the sheep and
cattle, they were in better shape than he'd hoped.

"Twill be a jewel once it's done," Malcolm said as
Jamie surveyed the view they'd just cleared. Luckily,
most of the valley had remained unobstructed through
the decades of abandon. They'd only had to remove a
copse of oaks and birch circling one side of the left wall
to display the river that wound through the valley. It
glittered in the sunlight; a blue-green gem filled with
fish that would sustain them during the lean years.

Malcolm's eyes ascended the stark white tower at
Jamie's back. "Ye think there's any truth to the curse?"

Jamie glanced at the pristine stone and shrugged.
Of the entire castle, it alone needed no repairs beyond
the door at its base. With the sun slanting behind it, he
could envision the renowned beauty who'd captured his
ancestor's attention to the extent he'd risked kidnapping
her. "Mayhaps. Or perhaps she's just waiting for
someone to rescue her."

He turned back to lift his ax when the chittering of

a hen harrier sliced the air. Malcolm's head cocked, and Jamie reached for his dirk. A second call came right after, and his grip lightened. Both turned toward the sound.

"Jamie, me boy, I think we've a wee problem." Jock strode toward them, his bow-legged gait chewing up the air, a concerned wrinkle to his brow.

"What kind of wee problem?" Had it been serious, Jock would have been running and there would have been a single harrier call.

The silver-haired man's face twisted, and he stopped to rub the back of his neck. "Well... it's a wee bit difficult to explain... Mayhap ye should see for yerself."

Without waiting for a response, Jock rotated and headed back toward the castle, tartan swinging like he was dancing a jig. After sharing a puzzled look, Jamie and Malcolm followed.

As they crossed the ground where the castle garden had been, a sliver of doubt tightened Jamie's shoulders. Neither Logan nor Ramsay were anywhere in sight. Crows picked amidst the overturned dirt, then scattered as the group approached, screeching with rage. A quick glance skyward eased his worry. Far overhead, a golden eagle soared.

Gaining on the elder man, a pronounced silence nagged at Jamie. Paddy and Niall were tasked with sharpening axes and repairing horse tack, yet the air betrayed no signs of metal scraping or Paddy's usual lyrical whistle.

As they approached the keep, Rory's chatter lifted on a smattering of laughter. An answering feminine lilt tickled through Jamie, instantly resulting in an annoying tingle in his groin.

The door to the hall gaped wide and beams of sunlight cut the newly replaced threshold. Jock stepped to the side and waved his hand, brows knitted and lips pursed with displeasure.

As Jamie strode into the doorway, his shadow fell over Sarah and Rory, and both smiled up at him. His stomach flipped. A jolt of lust hit so hard he had all he could do to stay on his feet.

Water pooled about the two small figures, soap suds creating clouds of iridescence around them. On her hands and knees, ass pointed in the air, Sarah wiped a hand over her forehead to push back a curl. The threadbare breeches and Rory's spare shirt clung to her curves, totally soaked and exhibiting every swell and dip.

"We're scrubbing the floor, Laird," Rory informed him.

Sarah sat back on her haunches. Pert nipples stood out, tiny pebbles begging him to suck them. His prick jumped, and blood pounded in his ears. Then she smiled, the sweet innocent smile that made his heart want her as much as his prick did.

"I'm not sure we're doing it right." Doubt riddled the words, but her face beamed as her gaze circled the room. His followed. Paddy, Niall, Logan and Ramsay stared at her. Wide-eyed, they looked like hungry sea-eagles perched above a school of fish.

"They've been fetching water for us," she added, oblivious.

Fetching water? Were they daft?

He cleared his throat, but a wave of anger choked him. One by one, men's attention shifted. Crimson washed over Paddy's freckles, and his eyes lowered. Logan, the only one who had ever seen Jamie truly mad with rage, raised his hands. Palms out, he dropped back a step. Even Ramsay, who feared no one, swallowed hard and looked away.

As his gaze collided with Niall, the ire crested. Niall's normally ruddy face blanched, but his dark brows lowered, as if the situation was Jamie's fault.

Jamie's jaw clenched, teeth grinding. Niall was right. This was his fault. Sarah didn't understand. She'd grown up sheltered. She thought an erection was a medical condition, like malaria or dysentery. The others didn't realize that. Only he did.

His hands fisted as tight as the lust gripping his loins. He should have been watching her, not chopping trees and bantering with Malcolm. This wouldn't have happened if he'd been here. Just as Joan would be alive if he'd not wanted to escape his responsibilities.

Malcolm's choked laugh bubbled behind him. The simmering rage boiled over.

"Out!"

No one moved.

"Now!"

Rory scrambled to his feet, then froze at Jamie's stare. Sarah's eyes widened. The men scattered in whatever direction offered an escape.

"Here. Ye'll need this." Malcolm's plaid swirled, and a heavy hand landed on his shoulder. "Don't scare her."

Scare her? He'd paddle her ass.

He stepped forward. Malcolm's grip tightened.

The red receded, then swelled again.

She didn't even have the sense to cross her arms.

Her breasts taunted him, nipples tight and wrinkled, the flesh above even creamier than if she'd been naked.

Another jolt of desire spiked through him.

He sucked in air and fought the wave of hot lust.

Malcolm's hold dropped away.

With another step, he spun Malcolm's plaid in the air. Worried blue eyes glistened as the wool settled over her shoulders. Tiny hands clutched the edges.

He forced his jaw to relax. Barking would only scare her, and her luscious mouth already trembled.

"I'm sorry." Succulent red lips formed the words. He didn't dare lean in to hear them.

He couldn't just leave her here though. He stretched out a hand.

Hesitant, she reached for it and started to rise. Her foot slid out. Soapy water sprayed. A choked gasp split the air.

With a curse, he scooped her up, along with the pounds of wool covering her. The scent of flowers wafted over him.

Hell, she'd put lavender in the water!

He shook his head and concentrated on his footing. Slick and treacherous, the floor slid beneath his foot. He glanced at the slick surface.

The entire floor was under water. Spotted rainbows of color winked at him, drowning in puddles of muddy water.

What a mess! The woman had no sense at all.

Jock peeked around the door jamb, brow creased. Their gazes connected.

"Get them back in here." Jamie picked his words as carefully as his steps. "Get this cleaned up. Whatever they were supposed to be doing had best be done before

I see them again." Maybe it would be long enough that he wouldn't kill them.

"Aye, Laird." Jock inched forward. "Come here, boy."

Rory scrabbled, wide-eyed, toward Jock's extended hand. He looked ready to burst into tears.

Instead, Rory lifted his chin. "Twas my fault," he said with just a trace of a tremble. "She wanted to help. Please don't make her leave."

Pride tempered Jamie's ire, and he drew a deep breath. Lavender and soap choked him. He'd never enjoy the scent again without remembering.

"Ye two did nothing wrong." The words didn't resonate as much as he'd hoped, despite the truth in them. They hadn't, but the effect remained.

His men had seen her as near to naked as a woman could get. And they'd reacted like normal red-blooded men. He himself had almost fallen on her like a lust-crazed adolescent.

Fear lodged in his throat. He trusted his men with his life. Always had. But what would they have done had Jock not fetched him? He wasn't sure.

"Sarah and I need to talk."

It was time someone explained the strange affliction she'd noticed.

Chapter Six

"Don't ye dare move until I return."

Sarah swallowed hard, staring at the finger lashing toward her eyes, and struggled to find her footing. Her leg ached and her knees burned from the caustic soap, but somehow, she maintained her composure.

It wasn't the first time she'd seen Jamie angry. More often than not he glared at her, and she'd heard him scream at Malcolm when a falling tree barely missed Ramsay. He barked when someone didn't follow orders and paced when she refused to answer his, but she'd never seen the fury-laden gaze he'd turned on them moments ago. It reminded her of Hammond's bitter scrutiny before he began another *penance session.*

Unlike Hammond, Jamie spun on his heel and strode toward the door.

"I'll be back when I've calmed myself." The door shuddered, flung so hard it nearly snapped the newly hung hinges.

Sarah choked back a sob and resisted the overwhelming urge to sink into a puddle. Perhaps if she did what he said and didn't move, he'd merely banish her. It would hurt ever so much more if he hit her. Hammond's age had weakened his muscles, assuming he'd ever had them, and she'd never seen him use them the way Jamie did. But it wasn't just the power behind

Jamie's fist that would hurt.

She'd never cared what Hammond thought of her. His insults had been mere words, his blows nothing more than pain.

She blocked out the image of Jamie's knuckles colliding with her face, his eyes burning with revulsion. A bubble of fear erupted. Where would she go? Who would take care of her?

You're a Clinton and a Campbell.

The litany started.

Clintons don't beg and Campbells don't cower. They're strong and smart.

A trickle burned her cheek, and she swiped it away.

Clintons don't cry. They fight.

Her father's words ran through her mind. She focused on them and the deep breaths he had taught her to hold back the fear.

She'd done nothing wrong.

But what if she had?

She scoured her mind. What mistake had she made? Had she caused trouble without meaning to, like the time she told Momma that Uncle Alex was coming to visit? Sarah's spine convulsed at the memory and pushed it away. Eilidh had locked her in the closet for days her mother had been so agitated.

Be brave. You're a Clinton and a Campbell.

But what had she done? Would Jamie tell her? Or would he insist she knew as Hammond and Eilidh always claimed? Would he, too, call her the devil's spawn?

Frustration welled up and stuck in her throat, like a chunk of chicken not chewed well enough. She'd tried so hard. Why did it always seem the harder she tried, the more she did wrong? She just wanted to contribute. Rory had thought it a good idea. Had they used the wrong soap? Or was it because she'd asked Niall to fetch the water? But then Ramsay and Logan had stopped digging the garden to help Niall. She hadn't asked. They'd just started doing it.

Shouldn't they be punished, too, if mopping the floor was wrong?

For what seemed like hours, she stood there, ignoring the ever-increasing burn spreading along her knees and hands. Over and over, she alternated between shoring up her courage, wondering what she'd done wrong, and convincing herself that it wasn't her fault. Her hands fisted, raw from the lye, but she resisted the urge to cross and rinse them in the basin of cool water Jock brought in each morning. She didn't think he'd mind, but Jamie had said not to move, so she wouldn't. She'd stand here until the soap dried to slivers of fire before she'd move. She'd not risk doing anything, for fear it was the wrong thing.

By the time the door swung open, her muscles and skin burned as brightly as her intention to live up to her name. Whatever the punishment, she'd not let Jamie see the hurt and fear.

But when she lifted her head, every thought flew away except one.

She'd die if he sent her away.

He'd bathed. His damp hair kissed his jaw as dark as honey, and his shirt stuck to his chest, revealing every ripple as he scrubbed the water from his nape. Her own muscles threatened to melt beneath the heat the sight of him created.

"Ye've not moved?" Confusion twisted his face,

lowering his brows.

"You told me not to."

The towel stopped moving, and he cocked his head. "I dinna mean ye shouldn't move at all." He strode forward, tartan swirling around his knees. Mint and spice drifted toward her. "Your leg must be in agony."

"It's fine."

"Ye dinna lie verra well." His lips pursed, and his head shook.

Sarah inhaled, her fingers itching to reach out and capture the lock licking his nape.

She shivered when he reached out and stroked her arm. It ripped through her, unlocking the joints that had frozen. Her knee buckled.

"Ack, sit down, *aingeal.*" He led her to the makeshift bed and supported her by the elbow until she sank to the straw mattress. "What am I to do with ye?"

Suddenly, the rules seemed silly. The urge to cry beat at her. She didn't feel strong or smart, and she didn't want to fight. "Please don't send me away."

The tears leaked out when he cupped her cheek. His face contorted, filled with the pain he was about to inflict.

"I told ye. Ye can stay as long as ye need."

A hiccup filled her, acidic and vile. She wouldn't make it any harder for him. "I understand. I'll leave as soon as I'm able. May I stay until tomorrow? Please?"

He chuckled. "Lass, I said ye can stay." His finger chucked her chin. The thumb that traced the tears down her cheek sent another quiver through her.

Then the words penetrated. Had she heard him correctly? She could stay?

His eyes darkened, and the play of his lips ceased. "We need to talk though. And tis not easy for me. Twould be easier if ye dinna cry."

He needed to talk? That was all?

"You aren't going to beat me?"

"No one will ever beat ye again!" He bounced to his feet and began to pace, hands clenched at his side. He looked as if he wanted to beat her, his bare feet slapping at the earth floor. "They'll not touch you, either. Not so long as I have breath in my body."

He whirled and pinned her with his gaze. "Twas Hammond Mitchell who beat ye, wasn't it?"

How did he know?

"And dinna lie to me, lass!"

Her eyes widened. "I…" She pursed her lips.

"Aye, ye were. Ye're playing with your hair again."

Her hand flopped to her side, and she grabbed it with the other.

"Sarah, tis time to be honest. I canna protect ye if ye are not. Hammond Mitchell beat ye, did he not? And you're a Campbell, are ye not?"

Her head shook. How had he figured it out? But it didn't matter. "He didn't want me." It still hurt. He was her uncle. He was supposed to protect her.

The laugh gurgled from his gut, sick and choked. "Aye, he did. Hammond likes little girls. He likes to hurt them even more. That *affliction* ye noticed proves it."

What was he talking about? "Not Hammond. Uncle Alex."

Jaime's head snapped back in confusion.

"He said they could have me. When Poppa died, he

64

promised to find me a husband, someone to love me, and then he left. I wrote to him. Every week I wrote, and I begged him to come and get me. But he didn't." Now that she'd started, the words came tumbling out. All the hurt and betrayal, all the grief and misplaced faith in the man who'd promised to protect her poured out. Besides her father, he'd been the only person who claimed to love her. She'd believed him, believed the promises he made at Poppa's graveside. Because she'd had no choice. She couldn't have continued otherwise. "He didn't want me. So, he gave me to them."

"*Mo neach beag gaisgeil.*" The endearment engulfed her, whispered as hands captured her face. "Ye've no idea, do ye?" Soft lips burned her forehead. She would have melted into him, had his grip not prevented it. Beneath the plaid, his thighs bunched, and he rocked back onto his heels.

"Sarah, when was the last time ye saw your uncle?"

"When Poppa died."

"Which was when?"

"Three years ago." Sarah swiped at the bitter trail of tears.

"And did he see ye while ye were in Scotland?"

"No." Sarah sniffled. He hadn't even cared enough to visit her.

"Was he aware your mother married Hammond Mitchell?"

"He must have been." She shook the question away. He was her guardian, and Momma's, too. Momma couldn't have married without his blessing.

Jaime's brow arched and uncertainty niggled at her.

"But I wrote to him." He had to have known. Didn't he?

"And who mailed your letters?"

"Eili—oh, God!" Eilidh, the woman who had punished her for making too much noise as a child, locking her in a closet and starving her. Eilidh, who looked so much like Hammond and told her no one would want her and Momma. Eilidh who had turned out to be Hammond's sister.

Their eyes met. Jamie looked so sure; so certain. But how had he deduced something she hadn't even suspected, not knowing who she was or where she'd come from?

"How…how did you know?"

"I'm a bard, lass. We're trained to memorize lineages and events. Took me time to piece it together, ye gave me so few clues, but when ye mentioned Eilidh, it began to come together."

"Is it a strange name then, Eilidh?"

"Nay. But tis obvious ye've led an extremely sheltered life, even for a Sassenach. I asked myself why. Then I remembered a Highland wedding from when I was a wee lad. I was only three or four, but it was the talk of the Clans for months. As a bard, my da went to the wedding, and he told me of it often. The bride was a Campbell, a beauty with hair the color of the sun. She had a maid named Eilidh. But twas rumored the bride was touched. Twas why the Campbell agreed to wed her to a Sassenach."

Touched. It was a kind word for Momma, for a woman who flew into rages for no reason and talked to unseen people for days at a time. Toward the end, she'd improved, to the point that Poppa had planned a quiet debut for Sarah's sixteenth birthday. But that had been canceled when they found him at the bottom of the stairs, neck broken.

The sadness weighed on her still. He'd been the only constant in her life, the only person who loved her. They rode for hours, speeding across the countryside. Until she'd broken her leg. Then he taught her to read, so she could escape to the places she'd never see. Uncle Alex had been the stranger who came once a year and played odd games with her and told her about her esteemed heritage. Then he'd started taking Poppa away when she was seven, leaving her with a houseful of servants for months at a time. She was just like her mother, her uncle had said, a princess destined to wed a prince. He'd watched her, though, with a scrutiny that unnerved her. It wasn't until she was ten that she realized they feared she too was mad, that they didn't see the friends who played with her. That was when she'd told her companions they had to leave. And they had until she needed them again.

Her friends helped her climb up on Romeo and reminded her of how to ride. They'd told her which way to go, that she'd be safe.

"Sarah?"

Her head snapped up. Jamie was watching her the same way Uncle Alex had.

"Have ye heard a word I've said?"

"Of course."

His lips twitched then spread into a smile. Heat rushed up when he wrapped his hand around the fingers twirling in her hair.

"What was the last thing ye heard?"

"About the wedding."

He nodded and laced his fingers through hers. Warmth spread through her, like when he held her at night.

"I dinna know what your relationship with your uncle was like, Sarah," he said, "but I know the man's reputation. He'd not ignore your letters or leave you in danger. And he'd not let his sister wed Hammond."

"He didn't know?" The relief trickled in, and a shuddering sigh opened the gates. She wasn't alone. She'd doubted her uncle's promises, but she believed this man.

"Nay. But he will, as soon as I send word you're here. He'll kill Hammond. He'll kill any man who touches you, so I need to explain something to you. Tis about the *affliction* ye've noticed."

Chapter Seven

"We found the pony."

Euanan glowered at the man but refrained from lashing out. Hammond would have, but he was better than his father. Hammond's methods didn't work, never had. Patience and cunning won the prize, not raw violence. "And?"

A huge ugly man, with the usual intelligence shown by his father's men, Boyd shuffled his feet as if he were no older than six. "We still ain't found the girl. Tis like she disappeared into the mists."

Euanan clenched his teeth and heard a crack. Incompetent. They were all incompetent. No wonder the Campbell had laughed at him when he'd approached with the idea of an alliance. *He* didn't want to be allied with his father.

"Did ye find *anything* besides the pony?" His gaze picked at the other three men. Like Boyd, they stared at the floor while another picked at a scar on his chin. The third hid in the shadows.

"'Fraid not." Boyd shrank back, and the scarred man tensed.

The third stepped out and returned Euanan's gaze. "There's one thing. Might not be anything though."

Euanan raised his brow. "Who are ye?"

"Duff, sir." He bowed. Finally, someone with a modicum of manners and a glimmer of cunning. "I

69

talked with the son of the crofters who had the pony. They said a group of Highlanders passed through."

"They didn't say nuthin' bout that to me." Boyd's mouth clamped shut when Euanan turned a murderous look on him.

"Go talk with them again. Find out who they are and where they went."

Boyd's ruddy face paled.

"He killed them." Duff sneered as he cleaned his fingernails with a tiny dirk. When he looked up, understanding shone in his black eyes. "I'd have handled it differently."

Euanan looked him up and down. Tall and wiry, the man returned the gaze with a hungry look. He'd bathed, and the sharp lines of his face were as hairless as a boy's. Soft ebony hair, neatly trimmed and pulled back, glistened above sharp cheekbones. A flicker of interest sparked.

With a wave at the door, Euanan dismissed them. "Duff's in charge. I want answers."

As distasteful as it was, he reached out and dropped a hand on Boyd's grimy shoulder.

"Not you. Da will deal with you." The look of horror almost satisfied Euanan.

****

Jaime watched the woman sitting before him, huddled in his best friend's tartan, and considered how best to proceed. Her gaze met his boldly, with an intelligence at odds with her unimaginable lack of sophistication. His own attempts to get her to open up had been futile, aside from two nights of whispered conversations in the dead of night. But he'd listened to Rory's chatter as he'd always done and watched the two of them and her interactions with the others.

Like a finely crafted ale, her spirit had bubbled up, leavened by the easy acceptance and innate friendliness of the group. He'd seen her explain Malcolm's calculation of the height of the tower to the boy, a technique most of the men had trouble understanding. Based as it was on the length of shadows and comparisons, it was math women rarely studied. He'd heard her discussing the properties of the wild plants with Ramsay and seen her examine the sloughed off skin of a snake with Rory without shuddering

When he'd asked Rory to try to talk less and listen more, the boy had surpassed his expectations. The expected result, that Sarah's long-bottled chatter would spill forth when tapped, had told Jamie enough to build the picture of her life.

Dark, enclosed spaces terrified her, yet she'd crawled into the crack of a mountain. She didn't ride. Her father had forbidden it after her riding accident, yet she'd dragged herself atop a pony to escape Mitchell. For whatever reason, her father had insulated her from the world. She'd had servants and tutors, but none had stayed long or cared enough to draw out the quiet child who'd learned to blend into the shadows. As a result, she'd devoured books and buried her need for companionship. She shared much of what she'd read with Rory.

"What do ye know of babies and how they're made?" he finally asked.

A puzzled furrow confirmed his suspicions. The connection between his affliction and the question was as wide as the valley the castle overlooked.

"I've never seen a baby, aside from the drawings in

my father's books. I know the anatomical details." She glanced at herself, her hands smoothing over the plaid covering her stomach. "I don't think I want to be pregnant. I saw Nellie when she had one growing. She looked like she'd swallowed a boulder. She said it hurt. But Cook fired her before it was born. She said Nellie was immoral."

He ought to use that as an opening but decided against it. Instead, he concentrated on the other statement. "Babies are wonderful. They remind you to see the joy in the world. You'd enjoy that." Just as he enjoyed watching her interact with his men. She'd beam with delight, just as she did now, her head cocked.

"Maybe. But does it hurt? It looked like it did."

"Sometimes. But not usually." Jamie turned away and crossed to add another log to the fire. The vision of Sarah blossoming with a bairn in her belly twisted his balls. His wife, Joan, had never been as beautiful as when she was pregnant. A petite woman, she'd glowed, her body softening into curves she'd never had. He'd loved her and considered her beautiful, but not in the same way Sarah was beautiful. Sarah's beauty hurt his eyes, the way staring at the sun did.

The fire flared, sparks nicking his arms. A smoky scent billowed and reminded him of the day they'd found Joan and the others dead. The grief had been nigh unbearable, settling so deep the thought of remarrying had been abhorrent. Since then, the idea flickered up on occasion, then was shoved down just as fast. He couldn't protect a wife and child. He'd had a chance and failed. He needed to restore MacIan Castle first.

Warm air licked his nape, and a shiver rippled

through him.

MacIan Castle would be complete in a year or two.

But he still couldn't protect Sarah.

The old familiar ache gnawed at his gut. He rose and turned.

Sarah leaned back on her arms, unaware of the effect it had on a man. The plaid draped over her, gaping where it hugged her breasts and flowing over the curve of her legs. She'd washed away the lye, and a pink tint kissed her skin. Her hair glowed, the shorn curls growing in and licking at her neck. Her blue eyes sparkled like water as they washed over his chest.

Her sultry scrutiny sent darts of desire through his stomach. His balls tightened.

"Lass." His voice sliced the air. "Do ye have any idea what the Mitchell wanted with ye?"

Her eyes flew up and widened.

Of course, she didn't.

"Of course. He wanted me to marry Euanan."

The response kicked him in the cods. He held his breath as the last missing piece fell into place.

She shuddered and pulled the plaid closer. "I refused to do it. As much as Hammond scared me, Euanan was worse. I don't know why. He never hurt me, and he was always a gentleman, but he terrified me. When they told me I had to marry him, there was no choice. I had to leave."

"Bollocks!" Jamie beat down the rage that flooded through him. Hammond's motives made sense now, and he wanted to process the information, but it had to wait.

He closed his eyes to shut out the nightmare image of Hammond or Euanan raping Sarah.

73

"What does it mean, tupping?"

Egads. She never should have heard the word. Or bollocks. How did women explain this to their daughters? They talked about love, but in this instance, it didn't come into the equation. Science hadn't worked. Sarah read books, but whatever she'd seen, it obviously didn't include the actual coupling.

Just tell her.

The voice wasn't his. Centered in his brain, the idea swirled, and his nape tingled, but the advice was sound.

"Sarah..." He drew a deep breath and just spit it out. "Remember the affliction you said Hammond and I share?" He didn't wait for her answer, and he didn't look to see if she nodded. "It's not a disease or a condition. At least not the kind you think. It's..." *Put it in terms she'll understand.* "It's how a man plants his seed in a woman."

A rustle told him she'd shifted position. He envisioned the expressions crossing her face. She'd suck in her bottom lip and chew it. Her head was likely cocked, and her brow furrowed.

"How?"

His exhale stirred the air, and the fire laughed when he opened his eyes. It danced in merriment. "Do you know how men and women differ... down there?"

"Of course. Poppa's books had many pictures."

Too bad he couldn't share her scientific impartiality. And apparently, they hadn't shown the male appendage in the enlarged state. Except perhaps when diseased.

"Well, when a man wishes," *and often when he doesn't,* "his organ...swells. When it does, he can put it inside a woman and make a baby." He dragged in another breath and rubbed the tension in the back of his neck.

Tu pourrais juste lui montrer.

The phrase wove through his mind, and he frowned. *You could just show her?* Since when did he think in French?

"And you want to do that? Put a seed in me?"

"Nay." He sighed, teeth aching. "It's not just about creating babies. It's complicated." He didn't want to terrify her, but he had to get across the danger.

"Tis instinctive," he continued, "to want to reproduce. So instinctive that when a boy starts to become a man, it swells whether he wants it to or not. Most men control it, but some don't. And some use it to hurt women."

A heavy silence fell, as thick and heavy as his cock had been when he'd seen her dripping with sudsy water. He was floundering. He barely understood what he was trying to say himself.

He dared a quick glance in her direction. She'd sat up on the chests Jock had pushed together and frowned at the flames, face twisted. Even her small feet wrestled each other, hanging beneath the wool blankets.

His throat tightened. How had she retained such innocence?

"Is that tupping? When a man does it to hurt you? Because Hammond's men used to say they'd like to tup me." Her chin trembled, and her voice dropped to a whisper. "Do you want to tup me?"

Dammit. What a muddle! And damn Hammond and his sick cronies.

"It's more complicated than that." Unable to meet

her gaze, he stared at the ceiling. "Tupping is just the term they use for when a man and woman couple. Has naught to do with why. Tis like saying a person is walking."

"I see." Her hand twirled at the back of her head, brows knitted. "So, you want to tup me, but not to have a baby or to hurt me?"

She was smart. Too smart to be so innocent.

He dragged in a huge breath and spit it out.

"Aye, I want to. But I'm a gentleman so I won't." He tugged a hand through his hair. "Tis not easy for a man to control the instinctive urge, though. And seeing a woman naked makes it harder. Sometimes, it makes them fight."

Her eyes widened when it registered, and she looked at where the linen outlined her bulging breasts. "Oh!" Her face pinkened like a sunset, and Jamie's loins tightened. She resembled a well-tupped woman with her hair licking her face, her complexion all flustered, and her clothes askew. "You're afraid your men will want to tup me? Because I was wet and my clothes clung to me?" Her gaze met his, filled with guilt and regret. "You're afraid they'll fight over me."

"Aye, lass." What he thought, that he'd have to kill them himself if they touched her, went unuttered. He'd made the necessary point.

Chapter Eight

Two days later, Sarah chewed her thumb nail and contemplated her situation while the men huddled around the table, pointing and scowling at the roughly drawn map atop it.

She didn't like it.

Rain pounded at the roof, annoying droplets sneaking through the ceiling to plop into strategic buckets. Smoke lingered in the air, unwilling or unable to escape the close environs, and the men were testy.

And where were Ramsay and Patrick?

Both had disappeared after Jamie explained the workings of the male body, a discussion that had left her with nearly as many questions as answers. Rory, who ordinarily answered any question, had just shrugged when she asked about Ramsay and Patrick. Jock claimed ignorance, as well, and the rest of the men gave her a wide berth, especially when Jamie was present.

Since the current deluge had started that night, it meant they'd avoided her almost the entire two days.

She glanced at the linen on her lap and smoothed the latest of the endless stream of mending she'd inherited from Rory. As soon as she patched one rip, another materialized. They smiled at her and thanked her for her efforts, but none of them sat and talked with her anymore.

And Jamie no longer slept with her. Her uncle would kill him, he'd said. So, she spent her days alone and her nights hidden in her room.

"We need more men." Carson's steady voice echoed the statement she'd heard more often than not. "The borders are too big. Hell, we canna even scout them all. We've holes as wide as Loch Lomond. We're all patrolling twice as much as usual. Sooner or later, we have to rest."

"I ken." Jamie kneaded the back of his neck, drawing Sarah's gaze along his nape and up his cheekbone. They all had circles beneath their eyes, but Jamie's reminded her of the black holes in the skull drawings she'd seen. "Tis just until Gus gets back."

Malcolm scoffed. "And if Bryan dinna send men? How long will it be then?"

"I don't know!" Jamie slammed his hand. The table rocked. The candle sputtered and splashed wax. He closed his eyes, and a sigh shuddered through the air. When he spoke again, his voice was soft. "I'm doing my best. I sent Ramsay to Bryan. At worst, twill be two weeks." His tortured gaze settled on Sarah. "Would ye have me hand her over to Mitchell?"

The chorus of nays warmed her, but not enough to fight the chill in the air. Wind whistled endlessly, along with the sporadic crashes of thunder that made them jump. None of them had slept for more than a couple of hours each night, thanks to the increased scouting, and the effort of pretending nothing had changed was wearing on them.

Why had things changed? She didn't notice any difference in how they looked at her. Logan still scowled before turning bright pink, and Niall still stared at her when she wasn't looking. Jock grumbled just as much as always, and they all nodded when she bid them good night. Malcolm was Malcolm, quiet and friendly in his brash way, winking at her when amused, but rarely speaking. She'd seen no signs that they viewed her any differently. Only Jamie had changed, frowning when someone spoke to her and assigning a new task every time they sat for more than a minute.

"I still dinna understand why we canna ask the MacDonalds for help." Logan stabbed at the table. "Twould cut down a quarter of the area we need to monitor."

"What would we tell them? The truth would open us up to someone leaking it to Mitchell. Anything else announces the fact we canna defend ourselves." Jamie shook his head. "Even if we can trust the MacDonald, we canna draw that kind of attention. A contingent of MacDonalds patrolling our borders would bring the Campbells down on our heads."

His eyes flickered toward Sarah. She chewed her bottom lip and dropped her gaze. The metallic taste of blood unsettled her as did Jamie's request that the men not learn her family ties. His reasons were valid. She didn't understand much of the Highlands, but her father and uncle had drummed the politics of it into her often enough.

Had her uncle massacred the MacGorans? The possibility twisted her insides. If he had, then he deserved his evil reputation. She didn't believe it, though. Her uncle was a God-fearing man.

Her gaze wandered toward Rory. Unusually quiet today, he sat at the table, chin in his hands, and squinted at the crude lines. Would his life have been different had the MacGorans lived? What would happen to him if the Mitchells found her and slaughtered them for sheltering her? Rory couldn't hide in a woodpile this time.

The sound of her chair scraping across the floor drew their attention.

"If I weren't here," she said, "would you be patrolling so much?"

"We're not giving ye back." Jock stepped toward her and dipped to retrieve the spilled mending at her feet. Logan and Niall grumbled in assent.

Malcolm straightened, head cocked, and shot a questioning gaze at her. "Why do ye ask, lass?"

She drew a deep breath and ignored their scrutiny. "If I wasn't here, you'd be concentrating on repairing the walls and putting in supplies for the winter." Like they'd done before she decided to scrub the floor. Since then, they'd done nothing but patrol. The rain likely prohibited some of the work, but the tone of the group had changed drastically, too. She might not understand why, but the effects were obvious. "You wouldn't worry about Hammond Mitchell or the Campbells, or anyone else."

"Aye, we would." She couldn't tell who mumbled it, but Jock and Logan nodded.

"You wouldn't be as worried as you are now."

"What are you suggesting?" Jamie asked, leaning toward her, palms on the table.

"You should do whatever you would do if I weren't here."

"Nay." He turned away as if the idea held no merit and focused on the map. "We canna protect ye if we do that."

"You can't protect me anyway!" Her eyes widened in shock as her shouted words echoed off the ceiling.

Jamie's spine stiffened, and his teeth ground so tightly she heard the grind. "You're right." Resentment filled the words, as deafening as her uncharacteristic outburst. "We canna."

Sarah's shoulders slumped. He hated her. For making him risk everything.

"She might be right." Her gaze jumped. Malcolm's hand dropped on Jamie's shoulder and his eyes locked with hers.

"When you asked us to come here," he said to Jamie, "we all knew the neighboring clans could wipe us out. Nothing's changed as far as that."

"Aye, it has." Still bitter, the words weren't quite as harsh, and Jamie's fists loosened. "Mitchell didna have a reason to wipe us out before."

"And as long as no one knows she's here, he still doesna."

Heavy silence settled, broken only by the incessant dripping. Jamie's eyes roamed over the map lines.

"Laird?" The worry in Rory's voice sent a shiver up Sarah's spine, but everyone else ignored him.

"She'd have to stay inside." Jamie met her gaze and longing sliced through her. Uncle or not, she wanted him to sleep with her, hold her each night, keep her safe and cherished. "Someone will have to stay with her."

Rory jumped up and tugged at Jamie's arm. "We have to hide her."

"Aye, lad." Jamie jerked his arm away and surveyed the men. Each shrugged or nodded, just as unhappy as their leader.

Suddenly, a short, quick convulsive shudder shook Rory. When it stopped, his big brown eyes locked on Sarah.

"We have to hide her *now!* Lady Aalis says they're here."

****

"I'm sorry, lass," Jamie whispered as he released her quivering hand and surrendered her to the darkness. Despite her assurances to the contrary, he sensed her terror. Her responses were stilted, and the grip on his hand so tight it could have been lodged around his throat. Nonetheless, she stepped back, hugging herself tightly, his thickest tartan clutched to her.

With a deafening thud and a mighty grunt from Malcolm, the shelving unit slid into place. The tightness in Jamie's throat slammed into his gut, and with a quick glance at his men, he nodded. Hoarse, he stated the obvious. "She was never here. We never saw her. Her life—and ours—depends on it."

His gaze settled on Rory, who pressed his lips together and mirrored the nod. The others didn't worry him. They'd participated in enough tense negotiations with enemy clans to do whatever needed doing, but Rory was an unknown.

"I ken twill be hard, lad, but resist the urge to prattle. The less ye say, the less chance ye'll slip up." He strode over and squeezed Rory's thin shoulder, a movement that echoed in his innards. He should never have brought the boy. One tragedy per life was too many.

"I can do it, Laird."

"I ken." Jamie drew a steadying breath and met each man's eyes. Like frozen soldiers, they dragged themselves into position, shaking off the visible signs of tension as they went. Jock trudged to sit beside Rory in the corner closest to the inside door. Malcolm and Logan placed themselves between Jock and the door to the great hall while Niall and Carson edged into the shadows. Jamie rearranged the pots and tools on the shelves, shaking his tartan to restore a layer of dust. As ready as possible, he turned and paced.

When the knock came, a deep thunderous pounding, everyone jumped. Jamie swallowed hard and gestured Logan toward the hall entrance.

Minutes later, five burly men followed Logan into the room. Two rivaled Malcolm in size. Two were smaller, but scars lined their neck and cheeks, proof their size wasn't much of a disadvantage. The last equaled Jamie in size and form, but with a wiry, hawkish look.

Five. We can take them. If it comes to that.

Slowly, Jamie rose and swirled his plaid to give a peek of the dirk at his waist. "Welcome. Tis a nasty night to be out." As was the custom, he gestured toward the stew pot. In the Highlands, hospitality trumped clan allegiances, especially in inclement weather. Anything other than an invitation to share would raise suspicion. "Will ye stay and dry out, have a drink and a bite with us?"

His gaze fell on Sarah's bowl, and his breath caught. Jock grabbed the bowl and scooped a generous portion of stew into it.

"Perhaps." The hawkish fellow stepped forward, gaze sweeping over the group, assessing. "I'm Duff. We're searching for a girl. The Mitchell's daughter. She's simple and wandered away. He's very worried about her."

Jock thrust the bowl at the nearest intruder. "We've plenty as ye can see. Twould be a pleasure to have a bit o' company." He beamed a grin exposing his smoke-stained teeth. "Rory, lad, grab more bowls."

Logan lifted a jug of whiskey from the shelf and began pouring. Duff eyed Jamie, then swept his gaze over the room. "As I said, we're searching for someone. Have ye by chance seen anyone unfamiliar?"

"Aside from yerselves?" Jock asked, pushing food toward the others. Everyone but Duff took the proffered bowls and began to wolf the contents. "We've only been here a week. So, anyone's unfamiliar. But we've seen no one else." He stopped and scratched his head. "Come to think of it, we've not seen a soul since a good day before we got here. Waved at a farmer that last day, 'bout a day's ride east of here, but no one since. Which direction did ye say ye came from?"

"I didn't."

"Take your plaids off and hang them by the fire," Jamie suggested, picking up his half-eaten stew and watching as Duff began to circle the room. The man still hadn't accepted the food and drink, and his hand lingered beneath the folds of the black and green tartan draped over his chest. Black eyes darted from object to object, paused on the pile of mending, then continued, finally stopping on the map spread upon the table. He studied the parchment, then passed his gaze over the men in the room. He was counting.

With a half-shrug, their visitor waved at the air. "Might as well dry ourselves a tad." His smile sent a shiver along Jamie's spine. Empty looking orbs, his eyes sucked the light from the room before redirecting at the map. "You're new to the area?"

"Aye. The castle's been in my family for three hundred years, but they abandoned it about sixty years ago. I came into a bit o' money and decided to restore the place."

Out of the corner of his eye, Jamie saw the strangers shrug off their heavy plaids. Good. They'd be on an equal footing as far as protection.

"You'll want to guard this stretch," Duff said, indicating the line of hills edging the MacDonald territory. "And this meadow here"—a silver dirk flashed and stabbed at the clearing to the west—"is prime cattle grazing land. The MacDonalds will raid you, but they'll probably leave you enough to survive. Never hurts to have a buffer between themselves and the Campbells."

So far, the man had said nothing he hadn't deduced himself, but Jamie thanked him anyway. A glimpse of steel winked from beneath Duff's plaid as he turned toward the hearth. Unlike his men, Duff made no move to disrobe. Did he hide one weapon or more?

Like a dance, both men sized each other up, and the groups introduced themselves. Whiskey and conversation flowed, some drinking more than others, and time began to pass. Where did they hail from? Would others be joining them? How well did they know the area?

Duff asked the usual questions, thinking he learned more than he did. Jamie countered but gained no more than he gave. Log after log burned in the hearth, and the rain continued to pound down outside. Each leaky drip seemed to take longer and longer to hit the buckets until Jamie wanted to scream. Long after Jock cleared the dishes away, Duff and his burly henchmen remained. The reason for their visit remained largely undiscussed until Duff began to stalk the room again, poking into corners, handling tools, and kicking at the boxes along the walls.

Jamie wanted to pummel him.

"Ye say the Mitchell's daughter wandered off? How old's the lass?" Jock asked between puffs of his after-dinner smoke. His eyes narrowed as Duff rummaged through the pots on the shelving.

"Fourteen? Fifteen, maybe."

"What's she look like? We'll keep an eye out."

Duff rotated and eyed Jock. Then his gaze slithered toward Rory. "'Bout the same size as your boy there. With long blond hair and fishy eyes. Walks with a limp." He took a giant stride and glared at Rory. "How about you, boy? You seen her?"

Rory's eyes widened, and he stumbled back. "Me? What makes ye think I've seen her?"

Jamie forced himself to remain still, even though his gut screamed for action.

"A lad your age must like to sneak out," Duff said with an evil grin, "torture squirrels and bunnies. Maybe peek in the windows of pretty girls."

"I dinna do that kind of thing!" Rory's face screwed up, and he stared back at Duff boldly. "And I wouldna tell ye if I did."

Lightning fast, Duff's arm shot out. Rory's shriek cracked the air. A screech of metal followed, and Jamie's men surged forward. Caught off guard, Duff's men scrambled, fumbling for their dirks and claymores.

A knife winked at Rory's throat. His scrawny legs kicked, thudding against drenched wool, while Duff pinned the boy's arms to his chest.

"Have you seen her, boy? Tell me or you'll all die." His gaze bored into Jamie, directing the threat at him as much as Rory.

Jamie forced himself to breathe and raised his dirk to point at the man. The urge to fling it and hit him between the beady black eyes nearly overwhelmed him. "Ye sure ye want to do that, Duff? We've no quarrel with ye, and the boy said he dinna see her."

Rory gasped and squirmed. Pleading eyes pierced the darkness while a drop of red leached from the point of the stiletto dirk.

"Actually, he didn't say that." Evil black eyes bored into Jamie. "And who's to say every one of you isn't lying?" With a flick of his chin, Duff's men advanced. "We could kill you all, and no one would be the wiser. And if the chit's here, hiding, we'll find her that much quicker."

"Aye, ye could. Kill us all. But ye're wrong about the rest." Jamie paused. Duff blinked, then his eyes swept the room. Jamie's lips twitched the minute Duff realized the truth. Carson had stayed just long enough to be counted, then slipped out the door.

Duff eased the blade tip away from Rory's jugular.

"The MacGregor will hear you were here," Jamie said, "as soon as my man reaches him. And the MacDonalds will aid him in any requests he makes. Plus, I dinna imagine the Campbells will take kindly to having *their* buffer removed."

The contrast between Duff's ebony hair and pasty white skin deepened. He'd taken a risk and failed, but he wasn't ready to back down. "I've no quarrel with you. Let us search the keep, and we'll leave ye be."

Jamie squinted, jaw as tense as a drawn bow. They were at a standoff, but giving in too easily would set off warning bells. "Let the boy go."

Rory stiffened as the blade bit deeper, a strangled gurgle of fear hanging in the air.

"First, we search."

Jamie gave a curt nod, but fury surged through his veins. It was the outcome he'd hoped for when they allowed them in, but it left a vomit taste in his mouth. "My men go with them."

"If you wish." The dirk eased off, and Rory sucked in a breath. A rustle of fabric and clatter of weapons told Jamie the room emptied out, but his gaze remained locked with Duff's. Thuds punctuated the air for a time, then dissipated, until nothing but the hiss of the fire moved the air.

"You all right, Rory?"

"Aye."

Jamie glanced at him, proud that Rory's eyes matched his response. They burned with resentment and faith—undeserved faith in his leader. Jamie hoped his own eyes masked the helplessness surging through his veins.

A short while later, angry grumbles heralded the end of the search. Two by two, the four groups filed into the hall.

"We found nothing. The place is a ruin. Doubt ye could hide a rodent in it."

"You look in the tower?"

"Aye." One of the men shivered and peeked at Malcolm out of the corner of his eye. "He tried to scare me away. Said it was haunted, but I looked anyway. Nothing but dust and spiders."

Duff scrutinized the group. His men shuffled nervously. Jamie's men looked wary but bored, a facade that would prove lethal if he allowed it.

"Verra well." Duff sidestepped toward the door, Rory still captive. With a swing of his head, he gestured the men out. "I'll be out in a minute. Be ready to ride."

After the last one hurried out, Rory's feet found the floor. A meaty hand imprisoned him still, dirk poised.

"I trust you'll let us leave unmolested. Else the Mitchell will be back to finish you."

"Aye, I'll let ye leave. This time." Jamie flexed his jaw. He hated that he couldn't stop them. Not without too much blood spilled. He hated more that the only way to protect them was to threaten them with Bryan's might. "But twill take more than the Mitchell clan to run us out o' here. He'd best have enough to take the MacGregor and the MacDonalds out, too."

Duff frowned, but then shoved Rory forward. The boy stumbled, knocking into Malcolm and Logan before he found his feet. Niall and Jock started forward, but a quick chop of Jamie's hand halted them.

Wordlessly, they waited, Jaime's hand raised, while Duff slipped out and the clatter of hooves drowned in the rain.

"Logan, Niall, follow them."

"Aye." Logan swirled his plaid over his shoulder, tucked an extra blade into his boot, and a claymore over his back. "How far?" He proceeded to pick up Niall's tartan and a bow and arrow and passed them to him.

"Long enough they can't double back on us. Come back once Carson joins you." Jamie's hand shot out and locked on Rory's wrist as the boy tried to rush past him. "Not yet, lad."

With a quick nod, Logan and Niall exited, and Malcolm's mass moved to block the door. Jamie looked at Rory. The blood on his neck looked as black as Duff's eyes. "Are ye truly all right, lad?"

A small hand covered the spot. "Tis just a prick. I wasna scared."

Not as scared as Jamie, at least. The boy's gaze flew toward the shelf, and Jamie shook his head.

"Not yet, Rory. Not until we're sure tis safe." It took every ounce of Jamie's resolve not to rush over himself.

"But she's scared," Rory whispered, lips trembling.

"I ken." Jamie hugged the boy's frail shoulders, his own heart aching. "But we must bear it a while longer." His eyes met Malcolm's. "Think they'll be back?"

"Aye. They'll not stop looking until they find her." His lips turned down in the corners. "They killed the crofters. And the pony. The bastard couldna wait to boast about it."

Jamie inhaled, then forced it back out. Two weeks. They only needed two weeks. Less if Bryan hurried or Patrick located Campbell.

Chapter Nine

"Ils viennent, petit."
"They're coming, little one."

True to the words, Sarah heard the scrape of the kitchen shelf a moment later and air rushed into her lungs. The sliver of firelight widened, and she scrambled to rise.

"Merci," she silently responded. Her muscles screamed, then rebelled. Too taut from the hours of disuse, her leg refused to brace. Unwilling to show weakness, she clutched at the slimy wall and dragged herself to her feet.

Rory plowed into her, knocking her against the hard surface.

"I was so scared," he told her, skinny arms squeezing her waist. More words followed, so fast and furious she shut them out. Grateful for the support, both emotional and physical, she hugged him back and blinked away tears.

"Are ye all right, lass?" Jamie's quiet question interrupted Rory's stream of babble. He pulled the boy off her and reached out to grasp her elbow. The contact sent a jolt of heat through her, and her lungs shuddered.

"I'm fine," she lied and pushed herself upright. Her fingers locked around her plaid to prevent the telltale reach for her hair, and she lifted her chin. She wouldn't show how terrified she'd been. Only children feared the dark, and the cave was huge, not the tiny stifling closet Eilidh had always used for punishment. And she wouldn't tell them Lady Aalis had talked to her and sung to her when she started to panic. They didn't need a raving lunatic on top of a fugitive.

"Jamie says tis all right to be frightened. Only fools are not." Rory's fingers snuck between hers and the cloth. She clutched them back and forced a half-smile. How silly was it to cling to a child?

"I dinna think it's safe for you to be in the castle with us anymore." Her stomach dropped so hard it bounced back up to strangle her, but Jamie continued. "During the day, tis safe enough, but not at night. Ye'll have to sleep in here."

Alone? She had to sleep in here alone?

"Oww. Ye're squeezing too hard." Rory wiggled his fingers out.

Sarah's fingers recoiled into a fist. Her nails cut her palm.

"Can ye do that, Sarah?" Jamie glanced around as if they hadn't spent four nights in the enclosed space. "Tis warmer than the castle, anyway."

Warmer, but she hadn't been alone. "Yes." She choked out the word. Inside, she babbled with denial.

"I'll stay with her." Niall offered with an encouraging nod. Sarah's lungs resumed dragging in air as the men crowded the opening, varying degrees of worry lining their faces.

Jock and Rory volunteered as well, and Sarah's breathing evened out.

"Nay." Jamie scowled, and tears pricked Sarah's eyes. She couldn't blame him. Her presence endangered them. That he was even willing to let her stay was a boon.

"Jock and Rory will sleep in the kitchen. We'll leave the shelf open. The rest of ye will bed down in the hall. If Mitchell's dog-bolt flunkeys show up, ye'll hold them off long enough for Rory to slip in and trade places with me. I don't care how." The set of his jaw suggested he'd just as soon they killed them. "Jock and I will slide the shelf back into place behind Rory."

"I'll fight them, too!"

Jamie shot a stern look at Rory. "Ye'll do as ye're told. I'll not leave Sarah alone again." When his gaze shifted to Sarah, a flicker of anguish glowed then disappeared. His throat worked and his mouth opened, but nothing else came out until he spit a Gaelic term she assumed was an insult.

A murmur spread through the group, and before she knew it, the black space filled with warmth and light. Jamie continued to issue orders while Sarah stood aside, afraid to move, afraid if she did, she'd crumble into a blubbering idiot. When he finally pushed Rory through the opening with a final whisper, the shelf slid half-closed and he turned toward her.

"Come here, Sarah." The hoarse, raw sound surprised her. His arms opened wide and welcoming, but her feet wouldn't move.

"I'm fine."

His eyes squeezed shut. "Tisn't for ye, *Aingeal*. Tis for me. I need to hold ye."

Chapter Ten

Relief flooded Jamie when Gus rode in two days later. Hooves pounded in the courtyard beneath the weight of six more Highlanders and their assorted gear. A chorus of greetings and back slapping followed as familiar faces surrounded the group.

"Bryan wanted to come," Gus told him with a grin. "But Jessica's beginning to waddle like a duck. Told him if he left her when she's six months along, he best not return."

A weak smile lifted Jamie's lips. Jessica's pregnancy had been one of the reasons he left a year earlier than he'd planned. Watching Bryan and Jessica together had hurt. When she'd blossomed with his friend's bairn, it reminded him too much of Joan.

Joan had never had Jessica's courage and strength, though. If she had, she would have demanded he stay, and he would have. She'd have lived, and his boy would be the same age as Rory. His life would be totally different.

The thought lifted his gaze toward the tower that reached for the sky. Sunlight bounced from the walls, slipping into the arrow slits. A dove took off, its silver wings winking back at him.

He would never have bought the castle, would never have met the MacGregor. He would never have found Sarah.

Sarah, who needed him in a way Joan never had.

Surveying the chaos, the dread lifted. Bryan hadn't come, but he'd sent a force to make up for it. Six of his strongest, slyest, fastest warriors now mingled amongst Jamie's men. A murmur lifted on the air, deafening in its promise.

"We ran into Ramsay on our way here." Gus ruffled Rory's hair as the boy grabbed his mount. Foam speckled the chestnut's snout. "Pushed ourselves after that. Figured you might need us here sooner rather than later." Gus scrutinized the group. "Where's Paddy and Jock?"

"Jock's inside. Paddy's delivering a message for me."

"To who?"

"I'd rather not say."

Gus's brow lifted. "You found out who she is?"

"Aye."

"Tis it going to be a problem?"

"Perhaps." Jamie's gut clenched. Given a choice, he'd not ally himself with Alexander Campbell. Not at the cost of Bryan's friendship and protection and setting the MacDonalds against him. But letting Sarah go unprotected wasn't an option. Alexander's wrath would fall on him if he failed to protect her, just as Campbell would exact revenge on Mitchell. Besides, honor demanded it.

Gus's half-shrug betrayed a lingering curiosity, but he turned toward the courtyard. "Jessica's sending clothes, but twill take a few days to get here. Oh, and I sent Irving and Keith to find Carson. Ramsay said the Mitchell border needed eyes on it, so I assumed Carson would be there."

Irving and Keith, too? Eight men total?

He exhaled. He'd always considered Bryan and Malcolm to be God's gift to him in exchange for Joan's death. This proved it. No one but Bryan would help an unknown, untested laird defend a piece of useless land in the center of warring clans. And no one but Malcolm would have left a laird like Bryan to help a friend revive a dead clan.

"No clothes?" Malcolm sidled up to look over Jamie's shoulder. "I'm not sure the lass can stand another few days. She's already itching like she sat in a briar patch."

"Aye." Jamie sighed. He'd cut her silk shift off the first night when he checked her bruises. Since then, she'd worn Rory's or his shirts with the leather breeches she'd escaped in or a plaid wrapped around her. Her pampered English skin had suffered even before the lye burns. With nothing but sponge baths, her arms and legs were raw and irritated. Yet she'd never complained.

Carson's last report said Mitchell was regrouping, concentrating their search toward the north, near the Campbell border. Gus's group had come in from the east.

"Get the men settled," he told Malcolm, "then come see me. Bring Logan and Niall with you."

Twas time he stopped believing in curses and started taking chances.

****

"Come along, Sarah." Jamie pulled at her hand as he led her through one of the tunnels that afternoon. The grin on his face when they'd started was infectious, but she couldn't share in his joy now. The ceiling was too close, the darkness too solid. Rory's endless chatter from behind her bounced off the walls, sucked up by the slimy moss and a trickle of water beneath her feet.

Oh, what she would give for a decent pair of shoes!

"Where are we going?" A sliver of fear shot through her, tamped down immediately. Jamie had said she could stay. He'd promised to protect her.

Poppa always promised to come home, too. And Uncle Alex had promised a duke or a prince for my husband.

"Tis a surprise!" Rory bumped into her, his excitement palpable. For the last hour, he'd bubbled with joy. A similar, tempered exhilaration galvanized Jamie. She'd chalked it up to relief at the arrival of the MacGregor's men.

"We're almost there." Jamie slowed, giving her a chance to catch up to his overly long strides. Sure enough, a faint glow penetrated the darkness before him.

"Twas me who found it," Rory informed her.

"Twas not, brat," Jamie corrected him. "We'd been using it for days before you found it."

"Well, twas me that found the tunnel to it."

Sarah rolled her eyes and hurried forward. Whatever lay ahead had to be better than groping their way through the dark.

Despite the faint illumination, Sarah collided with Jamie's back an instant later. As solid as the surrounding rock, her hand stroked the coiled muscles. Heat emanated off him, and the musky, whiskey-laden scent that wrapped her each night tickled her nose.

He spun around and grabbed her by the shoulders. His fingers stroked her upper arms, trailing sparks behind them.

"Are ye ready, little one?"

"Ready for what?"

"Your surprise, of course." His voice rippled with undisguised delight, and her lips curved up. Whatever it was, it was worth the wonder of seeing him carefree. "Ye must close your eyes."

"Very well." She squeezed her eyes, then allowed him to pull her in front of him. His hands settled over her eyes, then his body nudged her forward.

"No peeking. I'll tell ye when ye can open them." His breath snaked along her nape, and a quiver swirled through her belly. Behind her, the familiar swelling that plagued him at night sent another bolt of longing to her abdomen.

Step by step, he eased her forward. After the first few steps, the air grew warmer, then a slight breeze curled around her face. The smells changed, too, from the moist, decaying scent of moss and damp earth to a woodsy, clean smell. The sound of dripping water gave way to leaves rustling, birds chirping, and the gurgle of a spring.

Her breath caught. Outside? He was taking her outside?

His hands fell away, sliding to grasp her waist. "Ye can open them now."

Her eyes popped open, then widened. Perched on a ledge the size of a rampart, they stood above a glistening pool of water. A canopy of trees surrounded the pool, sunlight spearing through the waving green of elms and beech. Pine resin tinged the air.

"Would ye like a bath, Sarah?"

She swallowed, too overwhelmed to speak, as his

breath washed her nape. Her hand covered her mouth.

A bath? A real, honest to goodness bath?

"We can take you back inside if ye'd rather."

"No!" She spun, nearly tumbling backward, but his arms closed around her and pulled her back. His rumble of laughter surged through her blood.

"Truly? I can have a bath?" She glanced longingly over her shoulder. Blue beckoned. "Is it safe?"

"Ye mustn't tarry, and twill be cold, but tis safe enough."

Her joy faded as she peered down. It looked deep. Deep, and as blue as a sapphire. "I… I cannot swim."

A gentle brush brought her gaze back, and he pushed the hair from her eyes. "Tisn't deep. Rory can stand up in it. Comes to his shoulders, so twill cover you to about here." His fingers trailed over her collar bone until his palm settled against her chest, just below her throat. The touch made her breasts tighten.

"We all helped with the surprise." Rory wiggled his way around the two and deposited a pack he'd lugged through the tunnel. Two small hands dug into the burlap sack, then pulled out a lump of soap.

"Logan gave ye this." He held up the soap. Sarah lifted it to her nose. Rosemary, it reminded her of the steadfast man. "Niall wanted to give ye his, but Jamie said ye wouldn't want to smell like a pine tree." Next, he raised a bone comb adorned with carvings of mistletoe. "Jock wanted ye to have this, since he doesna need it much anymore." A pile of lambswool slipped from the sack. "Malcolm said ye could have this. He used it for wrapping his extra sword, but it should be good for drying ye off." Gingerly, Rory placed the pile on the rock and lifted one fold, then the other. Within the soft wool, lay a metal oval. He began to lift it, but Jamie snagged it from his hands.

"Careful, lad. We dinna want it reflecting the sun." Jamie held the object so Sarah only saw a wink of sunlight bounce against the mountainside. "Tis a mirror. For after ye've bathed. Carson's carried it about for years. He used to use it to signal us, but the enemy can see it as well as us, so we stopped using it. Well, except for Carson admiring himself in it now and then." He winked, and Sarah felt another of those strange stomach flips that plagued her whenever he was near.

"It's too much." Her fingers traced the carvings on the comb. Jock had told her it was his wife's. It and a locket he'd given her as a wedding gift were the only two items he had from their life together. She'd seen Malcolm wrap his sword in the lambswool. An expensive Damascus steel with elaborate artwork along the blade, the sword had been a reward for stopping the assassination of a French noblewoman. Logan's soap, while less valuable, held just as much sentiment as the rest. It was his mother's recipe, and she'd seen how much he missed her.

"Gus didn't have anything to give ye," Rory prattled. "But he and Niall are guarding the paths into the pond further out, and Malcolm and Jock are a stone's throw away. Jamie's throw, not mine. I canna throw verra far."

"Show her the rest. Rory."

Rory sat back on his heels and beamed his urchin face up at her. "Jamie always saves the best for last, ye ken." He bent and tugged a length of white cloth from the bag and exchanged it for the mirror.

"Tis going to be a bit big on ye." Jamie lifted the

garment before her. The width of his shoulders and the length of his torso, the shirt reached her toes. "But tis silk. My last one. And ye can wrap the last gift about ye like a kilt until ye have time to fashion a proper dress out o' it."

Her eyes widened and her heart stopped as the promised gift emerged. A rose-colored Lyon silk brocade, Sarah had discovered it in a chest one day.

"But..." She swallowed the lump in her throat. "Jock said it was for your wife." When she'd asked if she could use it, Jock had paled, then slammed the chest shut. He'd told her Jamie hated the fabric, that it was the reason he hadn't been there when the clan was struck down.

Jamie's lips thinned as he looked at it, then he sighed. "Aye, twas. But Joan was a practical woman. She'd have nagged me, called me a sentimental fool for keeping it so long. She'd want ye to have it."

The bright sunshine dimmed, and too choked up to speak, Sarah stood on her tiptoes and pressed her lips to his. It was just a touch. Jamie stood as still as a statue for the first few seconds, then his arm snaked around her back and trapped her against him. His forehead fell forward to rest on hers.

"Go bathe, lass. Before I regret the offer."

****

That evening, Sarah sat in her corner near the fire in the great hall while a din swirled around her. Jock and one of the new men, Gavin, prepared dinner in the kitchen. The rat-tat-tat of their knives created an underlying rhythm punctuated by random thumps and thuds. Across the room, Jamie and Malcolm argued with Carson and another pair, their voices rising and falling as they pounded on the table. Another group crowded around the hearth, rolling dice and laughing. The melody it created served as a counterpoint to Rory's endless rattle and shrieks of joy.

She'd never been in a room with so many people. The sound level was deafening, even in the cavernous space of the great hall, and the constant motion dizzying.

Yet she'd never felt so peaceful.

Her fingers stroked the brocade as she slipped the needle through the fabric. Somewhat tainted by Jock's contention that Jamie hated it, she'd still never received a gift that meant as much. That they'd given her so many wonderful, thoughtful gifts, for no reason, filled her with joy so great she feared she'd burst.

Her gaze danced around the room. Jamie's slow smile when their eyes met swirled through her until she looked away. Malcolm winked, and heat filled her face. Niall's protective study sent a shiver of awareness up her spine, and Rory's grin bubbled through her stomach.

Was this how love felt?

She concentrated her gaze on her stitches and pondered the question. She'd been happy when Poppa returned with gifts from faraway places or her uncle spent time with her, playing the strange games he liked, but somehow this seemed different.

She shifted and sighed at the slide of silk over her skin. The tune Lady Aalis had sung began to hum through her mind while the scent of venison and baking bread tickled her nose.

It was wonderful to be clean. The itchiness that had begun to drive her insane was fading, and the mirror had shown her that Jamie's assurance that her hair was still beautiful wasn't just kindness. In fact, she liked the riot of curls and how easy it was to comb out.

In and out, her needle whispered through the silky fabric, each stitch building on the last. One of the few skills she had, the garment came together with ease while the surrounding clamor fell away.

When next she glanced up, her contentment died.

Everyone stared, motionless and slack mouthed.

She glanced behind her. Nothing but wall.

Embarrassment flooded her as the silence penetrated. She'd been singing.

"I'm sorry." She clamped her mouth shut and clutched the rose-colored fabric.

"You're sorry?" Malcolm's brows arched, and he laughed. "Whatever for? Ye sing like an angel."

Her gaze flew around until Jamie's locked with hers.

"Where did ye learn that, lass?"

She blinked. "I had a tutor when I was little." She knew it wasn't what he meant.

He shook his head. "Nay. The song. Where did ye learn it?"

"I don't remember." Her fingers tightened. She wouldn't twirl her hair. "Here and there. Maybe Momma sang it." Her mother had never sung. She ranted and screamed, never sang.

"Lady Aalis sings it."

Sarah's stomach fell, and she glowered at Rory. She should have known he'd heard it, too.

"Is that true?" Jamie rose and crossed the room, his long legs gliding across the space as if it were empty instead of filled with numerous giants. He sank to his haunches before her and uncurled her fingers. A strange quiver ran up her arms and his gaze stroked her face with the same slow tremor the song created. "I've never heard the whole song," he said with a breath of awe. "Tis known as the Lost Lament. Only the tune and bits o' words survived. But ye sang the whole thing."

"I did?"

"Aye." His lips curled. Her nerves trilled.

God, he was gorgeous.

"Do ye know what ye've done?"

The lump in her throat refused to move, so she shook her head.

"Ye've solved the riddle."

She had no idea what he meant, but the murmurs grew, filling the silence.

She'd mimicked the words. They'd filled her head ever since she'd hidden in the cavern, but she didn't recognize many of them. There were too many Gaelic ones. "What riddle?"

"The riddle of why Lady Aalis is still here."

"You believe in ghosts?" Her gaze scurried over them. A few shrugged, others looked away, but no one shook their heads.

"Let's just say we dinna disbelieve."

Clinging to his fingers, she dragged in a breath of courage. The song had haunted her, a sad, lonely melody filled with Gaelic words. "What does the song say?"

Jamie rose and pulled a chair over with his foot. His thumb stroked the palm of her hand, never releasing it. He sat beside her and faced the group. Sarah relaxed as their attention shifted to him.

"Tis sad. It says she loved the laird, but they were

both too proud to admit it. She refused to come out of the tower until he told her." An anguished look lined his face. "Their eldest son fell from the window when he was two. The laird trapped her here with the curse. Until the MacIan line rises to glory once again."

"Oh." Sadness filled Sarah. How long had Lady Aalis been trapped, alone in the tower that had taken her son? Without the man she loved? It was awful. Almost as horrible as the MacGoran Lament.

Jamie's lips touched her knuckles, and the butterflies whirled up her throat. "Don't be sad, Sarah. At least we can release her now."

Malcolm's wry laugh paralleled Sarah's sentiments. "Aye. Ye just need to build a clan to rival the Campbells and MacDonalds whilst squeezed between the two of them. Shouldna be hard." Another humorless chuckle rumbled up. "That or ye could mate with Sarah and father a bard so great its voice cracks the tower. Twould be easier, I think."

The glower Jamie shot at him told her the likelihood of *that*.

Chapter Eleven

"What's troubling ye, lass?"

Jamie shifted uncomfortably beneath the covers and squeezed his eyes shut. Every touch of her silk-clad curves drove him crazy. The restlessness had started as soon as they retired, and two hours later, she still squirmed every few minutes.

"Nothing."

His eyes rolled, and he slid a comforting hand along her arm. "Dinna make me beg. Tis obvious your mind is tumbling about in that pretty head of yours. Tell me what it's chewing on."

The crackle of the fire highlighted the silence and reflected off the blonde curls. Even more gold than he'd imagined, the bath had polished the downy strands. His loins tightened. The bath had been as bad an idea as the silk shirt. The glimpse he'd stolen as she rose from the water burned in his mind. More nymph than angel, the vision taunted him with the promise of hidden treasures.

Treasures he'd never enjoy.

"I was just wondering."

Reluctant, he lifted his head and gazed at her. She stared into the flames, chewing her bottom lip. The lip he wanted.

"Did you love her very much?"

He blinked. "Who?"

"Your wife. Joan, wasn't it?"

Not at all what he'd imagined, the topic did what he hadn't been able to do himself. It doused the desire licking at him.

"I did." Ghostly flashes of their life formed in his mind; the first day he'd seen her, the day they stood at the altar exchanging vows, the sight of her pushing his son into the world. Bittersweet, the images no longer stabbed him. They'd faded to a dull ache.

"How did you know you loved her?"

"I always knew." Why was she asking? "The first day I saw her I knew I would marry her. We were eight and ten, but I knew." A smile tickled his lips.

"How?"

"Joan told me. She was older and much wiser than I, a fact she reminded me of every chance she had." His laugh vibrated through him. She'd needed to believe it, and he'd let her.

"She sounds…nice."

He swallowed the next laugh. Now that Sarah's face showed clearly, the furrow in her brow betrayed her lie. She hadn't reached for her hair, though.

He frowned as worry snaked through him. Did she imagine herself in love with him? She wouldn't be the first young girl to do so. Best to assume so and prepare her just in case. Her uncle would never accept a match with him.

"Joan was practical and determined, and she loved me with a fervor that awed me. In hindsight, tis clear I didn't deserve it."

Instead of reassuring her, the proclamation darkened her face further. "She was lucky. You were, too." She buried her face in her arm, but not before he saw the glimmer of a tear.

"What's wrong, *le-*" He bit off the Gaelic endearment. Calling her sweetheart would only encourage any romantic thoughts she had. Instead, he ran a soothing hand along her back. "What's upset ye, Sarah?"

"It's silly." Muffled by folds of silk and wool, he strained to hear her words.

"Tell me anyway."

She flipped onto her back. A silky leg brushed his crotch and lust flared anew.

"I understand how it works." She gazed at the ceiling, lips tight with unhappiness. "I know my uncle will wed me to someone for political gain. I know that if I'm lucky, he'll choose someone young and hale, and that I might learn to love him, but he might not. My uncle might pick someone old and mean, or someone who won't care for my happiness. I've always known that, and I never questioned it. Not even when I read *Romeo and Juliet*. But now I know it isn't always like that. It wasn't for you, and it wasn't for Lady Aalis. It makes me want more."

Jamie swallowed the trite denial he wanted to utter. Every word was true, and they both knew it. If he told her Alexander would choose well, that she might love whoever he picked, they'd both know he was just trying to appease her.

"Would you kiss me, Jamie?"

His loins clenched, and he stopped breathing.

"Just once? So, I'll know what it's like?"

Holy Mary, Mother of God!

"I can't." Hoarse and low, he hardly heard the words himself.

Her lip trembled, and she threw herself back onto her side. "I told you it was silly. I knew you wouldn't want to." Her hand swiped at her cheek. "I should have asked someone else."

His arm lashed out as she started to scoot away.

"Like hell, ye will." He dragged her back and pinned her beneath him. Her eyes widened into deep blue saucers. He made no attempt to hide the raging erection pressing into her. "Ye realize," he ground out, "your Uncle will kill me for this, do ye not?"

Her eyes caressed him, and her throat rippled. "I won't tell." Hushed and breathless, her tiny pink tongue darted out to moisten her lips, and his last bit of willpower dissolved.

With one quick move, he slid one arm beneath her waist, one hand behind her head, and flipped her atop him.

Her slight weight covered his front, tense until she realized his intent. Then her body flowed over him, and her arms relaxed. A question lit her eyes.

"You've no idea how long I've wanted to do this," he told her, his voice surprisingly hushed. Her lips curved, a slow smile blossoming across her face, and for once, he allowed himself an unhurried, purely selfish look.

She was liquid sunshine. Her riot of curls blinded him with their gleaming white gold. Her eyes warmed him like a cloudless summer day, and her skin glowed like a field of sun-kissed white heather. As his gaze stroked her, he watched the play of emotions, the gentle wash of pink that brightened her cheeks as he stared into her eyes, the quick intake of breath when he studied the gentle curve of her mouth, the dip of her gossamer eyelashes when his scrutiny overwhelmed her.

His neck strained to reach the succulent lips that reminded him of the more common pink heather. A pale dusty rose, they were anything but ordinary, and he'd wanted to taste them for so long he ached with it. The line of them bowed perfectly, and when she laughed, all he heard was the lilt of a harp.

Had she really never been kissed?

She went still as his lips touched hers, proving it. As light as a whisper, he brushed his lips over hers and held his breath. Experience hadn't prepared him for this. In the past, encounters had always been with women fully cognizant of what happened between a man and a woman. Even Joan had learned to kiss before he had, and together they'd navigated the physical aspects of marriage. He'd never touched another virgin, nor kissed anyone not previously adept.

And although he'd always made sure they left as satisfied as he, he'd never truly cared if they enjoyed his kiss.

Carefully, half afraid she'd bolt, he eased closer. They could have been clouds, her lips, so soft he might have imagined them.

With a sudden rush of air, she exhaled, and he drew back.

"Is that all?" Hands on his chest, she pushed herself up, but his arm locked behind her.

Laughter rumbled up from his stomach. "Hardly." His fingers tightened on the back of her head. "Ye've had but a taste. Tis a whole meal of culinary delights in a kiss."

Her eyes widened, and Jamie grinned as he pulled

her mouth toward him. His own mouth watered, and this time, he didn't worry about frightening her.

With a nip at the corner of her mouth, his tongue darted out. Her sugary taste tightened his stomach and convinced him to sip the other side. Just as heady as the first, he traced along the lower lip, trailing his tongue to capture every morsel of sweetness, every drip of nectar, every hint of flavor.

Sarah went still once again, and her breath slipped over him, seeping through the tiny slit between her lips.

Honey. Her breath smelt like lemon and honey.

He stifled a groan and inhaled, head dropping back. Kissing her was a mistake.

Sarah's throat rippled, and her lashes fluttered up. A crease of worry furrowed her brow.

"Is there more?" Her tongue moistened her lip, and she swallowed.

"Aye." With her slightly dazed look, he wanted nothing more than to continue. "But I canna. Twas too much already." Already the taste of her would linger, haunt him the rest of his days.

When she fell against his chest, he closed his eyes with a mix of relief and disappointment.

The relief was short-lived.

"What's it like? To be married? Is it like kissing?" As she asked, her hand grazed his chest, fondling the hairs that formed a vee at his stomach. Each touch sent a quiver of need through him, as intense as the desire to show her exactly what kissing should feel like.

Smothering the urge and quelling the ripples in his abdomen, he trapped her hand. "It depends. It's different for everyone. It can be easy and comfortable." It had been for Joan and him, in the beginning. "Or tense and difficult." Like when Joan had wanted him to join the Campbells and when she'd refused his bed after bearing the babe. "If you're lucky, it's exciting and fulfilling." Like Bryan and Jessica's marriage.

"Is it scary? Knowing you'll wed someone and never kiss another?"

Longing gripped him, twisting his insides, but he answered truthfully, if not honestly. "Aye. Tis terrifying. Because if it's the right person, ye doubt you're good enough, ye think ye dinna deserve them. Ye fear they'll leave or be taken from ye. You worry, every minute, that it might be the last time ye see them, hear them, touch them." Another shudder of yearning rocked him, and he stroked her spine, his fingers savoring the silken feel of her skin, absorbing the glow that fed her goodness. "Ye dinna regret that ye'll not kiss another. Ye dinna want anyone else."

When her neck arched to look at him, her eyes glistened with unshed tears. "Kiss me again, Jamie. Please."

His hand covered her throat, passing over the pulse beating beneath her ear. The thought she would wed another, be kissed by another, be subjected to the passions of another, tore at him. He'd not been terrified when he married Joan. Frightened a tad, but not the overwhelming, paralyzing fear he'd just described. That stemmed from thoughts of losing Sarah.

She'd wed another. Someone powerful and deserving, who could protect her. She'd smile and laugh at someone else, kiss and couple and have bairns. And, god willing, she'd forget him, the man who'd risked death for a tiny kiss of heaven.

Surely, the punishment wouldn't be any worse if he

had another taste?

He resumed his assault, bestowing another flurry of nibbles and kisses, his palms caressing her cheeks, his thumbs stroking the lines of her face, while he dragged the sweetness from her lips.

"Open your mouth, love," he murmured as his mouth traced the path of his fingers up along her jaw, pausing to suckle the fluttering pulse, then returning to the entrancing juncture of her lips.

He groaned as his tongue delved into the softness. Warm and moist, she tasted more intoxicating than mead, and her lips softened beneath his. It wasn't enough.

"Kiss me back, Sarah."

When his tongue dove back in, any hesitation vanished. With a breathy exhale, she kissed him back, tentative slips of a dainty tongue, mimicking the probing touch of his. Hungry, he slanted his mouth up, urging hers closer, breathing her in while his fingers caressed the silky, curl-topped curve of her head.

"God, ye're sweet." He moaned, neck straining while he pushed to go deeper. She fought him now, her tongue sparring with his, pushing and pulling between gasps and groans. Her silken hands joined the battle, sliding along his pectorals and clutching at his shoulders in a vain attempt to get closer. His skin convulsed with each touch. Fire streaked along the nerves, sending flames of desire to his groin.

"We have to stop." His mouth wouldn't obey, and Sarah didn't seem to want to comply either. Tiny sighs of pleasure battered at him. Somehow, his hands slid over her, down her back, along the curve of her waist, to clutch her ass. Drunk on her kisses, he gave in to the pleasure. Even with the plaid between them, the curves and softness of her flesh quickened his blood.

"It's too hot." Sarah lifted her torso and threw off the plaid. Silk winked at him, curving against her breast, and his mouth went dry. Her lips descended before his mind registered it. Instead of his chest, her fingers dragged along his jaw, her mouth and lips imitating his first kisses, teasing and exploring with devastating effect.

A long, low moan echoed through the dark. His own. Her lips floated away, and ragged breaths hammered his nape. He followed, unwilling to let her go, his hands flowing over her limbs, pulling her knees and snaking along her waist, then dragging her against him, all while his mouth made love to hers. Pliant and weak, she fell back against his arms, dazed, and stared at him with passion-filled eyes.

His cock leapt, struggling to penetrate the thin layer of wool between them.

He had to stop.

Instead, his mouth recaptured the pulse on her neck. Like a cornered butterfly, it fluttered and beat against his tongue. He sucked the throbbing vein until she whimpered. Lightning flicks of her fingers across his torso combined with her taste to send shocks of desire straight to his groin. Her hips ground against the bulge, instinctively demanding. He drove back up, rubbing her until she began to keen.

What the hell was he doing?

"We have to stop."

"No!" Her nails dug into his shoulders. His hands settled on her waist, forcing her to stop grinding. Heavy-lidded, need-filled eyes locked with his. "Please!

I can't bear it." She wiggled, eyelids dropping, panting, as she found the perfect spot. His cock throbbed, pounding with each pant.

"We can't, Sarah." He pressed his forehead to hers and shut his eyes. He'd already gone too far. But, damn, it felt good.

"Don't you want to tup me?"

His whole body shuddered. "More than ye can imagine." The very thought made his cock leap. She'd be like a hot summer day, slick and soft, and all woman.

"Then why can't we? No one will know." Her hands wandered over his chest, fingers tugging at the hairs, sending shocks of delight over his skin, while her mouth continued to batter at him with slow licks and moist hot breath.

"I'll know." He snagged her fingers, a mistake, because his knuckles brushed her nipples, and she gasped, arching. "Twould be dishonorable," he mumbled as he watched. Even through the silk, her tits pebbled, dark pink circles calling for his touch. His palms itched to satisfy her, savor the heavy weight in his hands, stroke them until it hurt.

Her head fell back, exposing the delicious length of her neck. "Please, Jamie. Just once. I want it to be with you."

His name on her lips undid him. With a growl, he reached for her. He devoured her lips and rolled her onto her back. Silk bunched beneath his roving fingers, pushed aside to expose the beauty beneath. As much as he wanted to see her, he needed to touch her more. He needed to feel the undulations of her muscles, the skin rippling beneath his touch, needed the gasps pelting him with moist air as he palmed one naked breast, then tweaked the other.

One hand shoved aside the plaid guarding her mound, and a knee slid between her legs. She opened, instinctively arching, hips bucking. His cock throbbed, eagerly coating a shapely thigh with slick desire. With a muffled curse, he jammed the tartan against his pulsing member.

He'd not ruin her. He'd give her what she wanted. What she so obviously needed. But he'd leave her intact.

Her hands clutched at him, fingernails frantically sinking into his shoulders, trailing heat down his spine before pressing his ass.

"Stop, Sarah." Hoarse, he pulled his lips from her and dragged her hands away.

She whimpered, mouth still all over him, until he placed a palm against it, struggling to slow his own heartbeat. When her frenzied pants slowed and she met his eyes, he took a deep breath. His heart raced, pumping blood through his veins with the force of a springtime river.

"I can't do this, Sarah." The anguish in her face nearly killed him. "I can't tup ye." She turned away, her strangled sob twisting his heart until he reached out and made her face him. "But I can show ye what it's supposed to be like." He sucked in a steadying gulp of air. "Ye must never, ever tell anyone, and when you're wed, if your husband doesn't…take care of ye…ye can remember it. Think about it and how it felt."

The thought of her with someone else ripped through him, tearing through the scar where he'd once had a heart, but he pushed the pain aside. Only a monster could use her without pleasuring her in equal measure. And even Campbell wouldn't give her to a monster. "But ye can never, ever mention it. Can ye do that?"

Her face twisted with confusion, and her hands trembled in his, like fluttering birds. "I don't understand. What do you mean?"

"Do ye trust me, Sarah?"

Her nod was instantaneous.

"Then promise me."

She swallowed, gaze glued to his, and whispered, "Promise what?"

He kissed her trapped hands, freeing one. "Promise ye won't touch me." He'd shatter if she did. He might anyway, desire pounded through him so hard at the thought of what he was about to do. "And promise ye won't scream." Somehow, he knew she would. His quiet, brave angel would be loud when she came.

"But I want to touch you."

Her fingers danced over his chest, sparks that shot to his loins, and his voice dropped to a tormented groan. "I can't do this if ye touch me. Ye must promise."

In agony, he waited, watching the tortured look pass over her face like clouds until her hand stilled, then reluctantly dropped away, and she uttered a hushed, solemn promise.

Certain he'd lost his mind as well as his heart, Jamie lowered his lips and bestowed a light, tentative kiss. Featherlight, he nibbled and teased and ignored the fire burning through his veins. Already fevered, he slowed things down, for both her and him, until their breathing slowed and he regained control.

Then he ramped it back up one touch at a time.

First, he ran his fingers over her skin while he kissed her neck. Then he traced her jaw with the tip of his tongue, watching the shivers as the air rushed in to replace his mouth. His thigh nestled between hers while he sprinkled kisses across her golden lashes and flushed cheeks. When she forgot and reached for him, he trapped her, lacing his fingers through hers and lifting them above her head. He made note of the touches that made her gasp and ripple and repeated them, adding sensation after sensation.

Determined to make it last, he wandered along her torso, licking and kissing each patch of skin. She tasted like sunshine and honey, a faint salty taste adding to the intensity. Blowing on her exposed nipple, he watched, mesmerized, as her entire body twisted, reaching. Trapped beneath his weight, she strained, using her torso to accomplish what her hands couldn't. Like water, her form danced beneath his in the instinctive search for release. When he pressed her belly, her muscles quivered, tiny waves of impending pleasure rippling out.

Softly, his mouth lowered over her left breast. She jerked, and her fingers clenched around his.

"Oh, God." Breathless, the hushed cry hovered in the air, and he laved at the delicious bud, coaxing her higher. Her back arched. His cock jumped.

When he moved to the other breast, another, louder cry rewarded him, and he smiled. His angel was as passionate and uninhibited as a dream.

He squeezed his eyes shut and moved lower.

One night wouldn't be enough. He knew it. But he wouldn't regret it. He'd remember this as long or longer than she would, and only regret he hadn't done more.

He released her hands and circled her waist. Slender and soft, his thumbs touched near her navel, and he dipped his head to tongue the small pucker of skin. Again, she convulsed, and he feathered kisses over the smooth surface surrounding it, moving ever lower.

"Jaime!" As much a whimper as a wail, she clutched at the blanket as he slid his hands beneath her and lifted her hips. Before his lips even touched her, she shuddered. When the moist heat of his mouth found the soft wet folds, she began to wail.

His hand clamped over her mouth. She jerked and stuffed her fist in the space. Her body began to spasm, one lovely tremor after another. His cock throbbed in unison, angry at being left out, while he savored her reaction. He lapped at her salty juices while his own trickled down his stem, and he sucked the swollen, throbbing nub that had his heart hammering with need. Lust pounded through him, kicking him in the groin, ripping at his core, but he fought it. This was for her, his one and only chance to show her heaven. His cock could go to hell.

Her body fought the sensations. She writhed and bucked, instinctively afraid, yet hurtling toward the unknown. He played her passion, licking and probing, easing off when she got too close, pressing back when the intensity ebbed. His fingers kneaded her ass, rocking her hips back and forth while he worshipped her with his mouth. Heady and sweet, he inhaled her essence, knowing it would be the last time. He relished her throbbing, moist passion, and for one tortured second imagined sinking his cock into the pulsing softness.

When he feared she could take no more, he slid a finger where his cock wanted to be. She screamed, a muffled, glorious sound that raked his spine, then she arched, tense as a gale swept sapling. He held her there, the heel of his hand pressing against her need until the muscles stopped contracting and the soft mewling sounds died away. When she slumped, eyes dazed, mouth slack and gasping, he gathered her into his arms.

He'd regret this. That was as certain as his name. But not tonight. Tonight, he'd hold her and imagine what might have been. If only she weren't a Campbell.

****

Cold woke Sarah. Slow and insidious, it crept over her languid, heavy limbs. She fought it, hugging the heavy wool blanket to her chest, her memory of the night drifting over her.

What had he done to her?

Whatever it was, it had left her languid. With a sigh, she curled up tighter. Her muscles ached pleasantly. Even her leg didn't hurt as much as usual. She flexed the offending limb and forced her eyelids to open.

A faint orange glow barely touched the darkness, so she let them drop. Early, it had to be early. The muffled noises beyond the shelf hadn't yet reached the point of activity.

Why was it so cold?

She rolled over. Jamie would warm her. He was always warm.

Her hand landed on bare ground, and a chill raced up her arm. Her eyes snapped open. Dark earth stared back at her, broken only by the trickles of moisture reflecting the orange embers behind her.

"Jamie?" Her eyes searched the shadows. Nothing. The silence sucked up her voice. She repeated it, louder.

A thunk sounded, followed by the shuffling of feet. A quick scrape raked her ears, then footsteps started toward her.

"Ack, *aingeal,* I'm sorry." Jock slid a log onto the fire. "The laird told me to keep the fire going, but I forgot. Go back to sleep." Another thick blanket floated over her, but did little to relieve the chill.

"What time is it?"

"Tisn't even dawn." His uneven gait headed back toward the shelf opening. The fire spit, and Sarah watched Jock slip out. The shelf closed with a thud.

Not even dawn. And Jamie had been gone long enough for the fire to die.

Sarah laid her head back down. Her leg didn't ache now. Her heart did.

****

Jamie and Malcolm crept through the forest, weapons poised. A sliver of moon lit the way, its glow penetrating the limbs overhead, but the darkness made every step difficult.

A muted crack caused Jamie's jaw to clench. Malcolm's size made stealth impossible. He should have asked Logan to accompany him. Logan liked to ask questions though. Malcolm would just sit with him.

The distinctive sound of a tawny owl rose, cutting through the air.

Malcolm froze. A second later, Carson's soft laugh broke out and Jamie whirled.

"I heard ye ten minutes ago." The dirk aimed at Malcolm's throat dropped away, winking in the moonlight.

"Egads, Carson. Why must ye do that? My heart stopped."

"Tisn't supposed to stop ye heart. Tis supposed to make ye use yer blade." His own knife disappeared, as silently as it had appeared, and Jamie's shoulders relaxed. Had they been in danger, Carson would have dragged Malcolm into the brush, hand over his mouth, and Jamie never would have seen it.

"Any sign of Mitchell's men?"

Carson shook his head. "Keith spotted them heading north last night. I figure we have another day or two before they redirect. Twill take them that long to satisfy themselves she dinna make it to the Campbells." Carson frowned. "What are ye doing here?"

Jamie shrugged. "I needed to do something. Figured you'd appreciate a couple extra hours of sleep."

Carson scoffed. The man never slept more than three hours, and the arrival of the MacGregor men already guaranteed he'd sleep as much as he wanted.

"It's been quiet. Irving's covering the south, and there's not much activity other than two groups that head out each day. Mitchell isn't exactly skilled at motivating his men." Carson's form, little more than a shadow, turned and moved between the trees. Jamie and Malcolm followed. After a few steps, Carson slipped atop a huge boulder, belly down. Jamie crawled up beside him.

A faint pink hue lightened the sky, casting a deceptive glow on the massive structure before them. Huge black towers pierced the dawn light, stretches of merlons and crenets forming the battlements between, giant black teeth gnawing on a red tongue. Far enough away that no one would pick them out amongst the swaying trees and looming rocks, the perch afforded an excellent view, but it meant the figures moving atop the parapet were unrecognizable blobs. Below, a gatehouse crouched above a gaping moat, a tiny sliver of a drawbridge bisecting the black water.

How had Sarah slipped out unnoticed? Expansive, cleared areas announced intruders well before they arrived, and hulking wing walls prevented entrance from the moat. Getting out had to be as difficult as gaining entrance.

Carson rolled off the boulder and strode toward a nearby clearing. "Ye can watch from here, too. Tis a tad more comfortable."

Jamie stared at the castle. The urge to kill Mitchell and his son, if not the entire clan, had been building since Duff had held the knife at Rory's throat. He'd hoped seeing the castle would expose a weakness he missed. Instead, it confirmed what he feared.

The only way to take Mitchell Castle was from within or with a force larger than his. Even the Campbells might not be able to do it.

"How many men does he have?" Jamie asked, then dropped to the loamy forest floor.

The last count had been higher than he liked.

"Two hundred and twenty-seven."

Jamie and Malcolm glanced at each other. Neither asked how Carson had arrived at such a precise number. It didn't matter. Half that was too many.

"Paddy needs to find Campbell. Soon." The statement sent a pang of loss straight to his heart. He'd wanted more time. But after last night, he no longer trusted himself.

"He's not a bad man," Carson said as he pushed a silver flask at Jamie and sank down to sit cross-legged on the ground. "I know what they call him, but tisn't for the reason most think." Jamie had told Carson about the identity of Sarah's uncle in case he spotted any Campbells entering Mitchell's keep. "Alex doesna agree with everything his cousin does and plays Devil's advocate. Tis where the nickname originated. Still, I'd not want to be Mitchell right now. Alex will show no mercy when he hears what he did."

"It doesna matter." Jamie tipped back the flask and let the whiskey burn. It chewed through the cold but hit the pit of his stomach like a rock. He'd destroyed any chance that the man would thank him for protecting Sarah. Even if he kept her safe until Campbell arrived, his actions had doomed him as surely as Mitchell.

"Christ's teeth!" Malcolm spit. "Ye tupped her, didn't ye? That's what Niall heard last night. Jock told him twas his imagination." He started to laugh, the sound rolling through the dawn until he caught himself. "That's why ye dragged me out in the cold of night?"

Jamie flinched. "I dinna." His lips curled in disgust. He lied as poorly as Sarah. "She's still a maiden."

Carson's brow quirked. Then he too began to chuckle, a soft, refined laugh that twinkled in his eyes. "I doubt Alex Campbell will appreciate the distinction."

Jamie scowled but couldn't argue. He'd drunk and wenched his way through most of the Highlands, and much of the Lowlands, with Carson. They'd even shared a wench or two. The man knew him as well as Malcolm, maybe better when it came to women.

Still, he'd hoped for silent support, not laughter.

He scrunched his eyes. How had he been so weak?

Carson's hand squeezed his shoulder and any remaining laughter died away. "You in love with her?"

Was he?

He sighed. "Does it matter?"

"Maybe." Carson extended the flask again. "The man wanted ye as his bard at one time. He must have liked ye."

"That was years ago." Before he'd destroyed the innocence of the man's niece.

"Still, if ye love her, ye should fight for her," Carson added.

"No, he shouldn't." Both gawked at Malcolm. "Well, ye shouldn't." He shook his head as if they were idiots. "I'm sorry to tell ye this, Jamie, but ye are not a fighter. Ye never have been."

Jamie bristled but remained silent. Not only was it true, but when Malcolm spoke, only fools interrupted.

Malcolm snatched the flask and took a long draft before continuing. Behind him, the sky brightened, the pink giving way to purple and blue. "Use yer brains. Tis why God gave them to ye." He swiped at his mouth, then spat at the ground again. "Why did Mitchell want her? As pretty a thing as she is, she's hardly young enough for his tastes. And his whelp doesna even like women, yet they're combing the Highlands looking for her."

"Aye, so he can force her to wed Euanan." They'd already figured that out. It was a power move, to force Alexander and his more influential cousin, Archibald, to ally with them. "Are ye saying I should force her to wed me?"

Much as he liked the idea, he'd already discarded

it. Mitchell was strong enough and feared enough to survive a Campbell war if it came to one. He wasn't.

"Nay. I'm saying ye should use what ye have and Mitchell doesna."

"And what's that? My famed voice?"

Malcolm rolled his eyes. "Ye've a reputation, Jamie. It's known ye dinna give your word or your loyalty lightly, and that once ye do, ye'll not break it. The MacDonald kens ye'll not raise arms against him, and if ye pledge the same to the Campbell and the MacFarlans, they'll believe ye. So will the Stewarts, and every other clan in the area. Promise them all that ye'll only war with them if they strike first, and they'll leave ye in peace. Everyone except Mitchell, that is."

Jamie scratched his neck. It was, in part, what had allowed him to risk coming at all. "How does Sarah figure into it, though?"

"What do Campbells want more than anything else?"

He scoffed. "Power."

"Aye. They want to be feared and have influence. Alex Campbell is in France. Most of the Campbells are Covenanters, but Alex has always been a rogue. What's he doing in France when he's a niece of marriageable age in England?"

Jamie's stomach knotted. "King Charles? Ye think he wants her for King Charles?" Alex had always favored playing both sides. What better way than to wed his English niece to the man who might one day rule both nations?

Good God, she'd never survive court. They'd shred her innocence and sweetness faster than they consumed strawberries.

"It makes sense. Twould give the Campbells an edge no matter which way the war goes."

And he'd just destroyed that chance. Alexander wouldn't forgive that. Jamie rubbed the bridge of his nose and closed his eyes. Every time he thought it couldn't get worse, it did.

Then Carson spoke, a laugh in his voice. "Mitchell pickled himself. There's no way Alex can offer her to the king after this. Alexander's gonna flay him alive."

Jamie shook his head. Malcolm nodded, a grin on his face. "Aye. Sarah's ruined. Was the day Mitchell packed her into whatever conveyance he used to get her here. No one would believe she's untouched. Not with naught but an insane mother and Mitchell's sister as chaperone. Twas likely what Mitchell was counting on to make Alex swallow the marriage."

Malcolm paused, took another swig of whiskey, then passed it to Jamie. "And that, my friend, is what ye use to win her. Assuming ye want her. Show Campbell a way inside that fortress, so he can extract vengeance, and I expect he'll give ye just about anything ye want."

Jamie's gaze slid to the impenetrable castle. "How do you suggest I do that?"

"I canna do everything for ye, Jamie. I told ye how to win her. The rest ye have to figure out for yerself."

Chapter Twelve

Sarah donned her new dress that night and stepped into the crowded kitchen just as Jock began to spoon a fragrant stew into the wooden bowls. The fine fabric fell in graceful folds, and Jock had found her a black ribbon to lace through the neckline. With no pattern and no Highland women to guide her designs, she'd had to go on memory alone. As a result, she'd crafted a gown similar to the ones her father had bought for her coming out. She wondered now if it had been a mistake. The bodice strangled her, compared to the loose-fitting shirts she'd worn, and she had to concentrate on not tripping on the hem.

It didn't matter, she thought as she wiped her nervous palms on the skirt. Jamie hadn't looked at her all afternoon.

A chair scraped then crashed to the floor.

"My Lady," an unfamiliar voice choked on itself. "Take my seat."

"Tis on the floor, Evan," Carson drawled.

Sarah glanced up as a hand cupped her elbow and drew her forward.

"Sit here, Sarah." With a flourish, Carson toed a chair away from the table and bowed. A pair of soft lips touched her hand. "Might I add, you look especially beautiful tonight?"

Her face heated, but glad for the compliment, she

lowered herself to the chair. If only Jamie would look at her like that.

She peeked at Carson. He reminded her of Jamie. Both men exhibited a style that put her at ease while unsettling her at the same time. Unlike Jamie, and completely at odds with his normal behavior, Carson had watched her all afternoon. At one point, she'd gone to look in her mirror, convinced she had a piece of food in her teeth, or a bug stuck to her cheek.

"Yer gown came out lovely, lass," Jock whispered as he plunked a bowl before her. A spoon clattered, and Sarah wrapped her fingers around the worn metal, unable to lift her eyes.

She felt strange, had the entire day. Most of it was a lack of sleep, but she'd been restless and moody as well. Every time one of the men came in, her hopes flared, only to sink when it wasn't Jamie. Her stomach was queasy, her nerves jumped at the slightest sound, and right now, the rosemary and garlic wafting from Jock's stew made her throat convulse.

Not in a good way.

"How did ye get out of Mitchell's castle, Sarah?"

When she looked up, her stomach sank. They were all staring at her. Except for Jamie. He frowned at a piece of parchment before him.

She craned her neck, but he was seated too far away to make out what he studied.

"I walked out."

He scowled. "But how?" He shoved the paper across the table and jabbed at it. "Where did ye get out? Was it the front gate, or is there another way in?"

"I don't know." Irritated, she poked at a chunk of venison. If he wanted to talk to her, he could at least have the courtesy to look at her. "I left by the main gate."

"And no one stopped ye?"

"No." Sarah scooped a spoonful of stew and stuffed it in her mouth.

She jumped and dropped the spoon when a hand touched her leg. Stew splashed on the table.

"Are ye all right, Sarah?" Niall leaned toward her, his voice low.

She swiped at the stew with the rag Jock tossed to her. "I'm fine." With effort, she managed a half-smile. She liked Niall. He brought her flowers and fed the fire for her, and he never grumbled when she needed something from the top shelf. But he wasn't Jamie.

"Ye can tell me if there is." His fingers tightened over her knee, then relaxed. She shuddered at the touch, as heavy as a lump of earth, chilly and moist. She shifted, but the weight remained until she shoved it away.

"Pass me some bread, Niall." Sharper than his usual requests, Jamie's regard skewered the man before scraping over her.

Her fists clenched. Nowhere near as low as the dresses her father had commissioned, the scooped neckline left her feeling half naked. Worse, it made her prickle and remember last night. Why had he made her promise to never tell? Had they done something wrong? Was that why he'd left? Was that why he wouldn't even look at her?

The lump of requested bread lobbed through the air. Jamie snagged it, then turned back to the paper. "Mayhap there are tunnels beneath it, like ours." His finger traced the map. Beside him, Malcolm shoveled stew into his mouth with chunks of bread and peered.

"Maybe. Tisn't that far away. The terrain canna be that different." With a meaty hand, Malcolm leaned forward and snatched Jamie's bread, grinning.

"How far away is it?" Sarah asked with a frown.

Jamie's gaze never wavered, but Malcolm's skipped toward her.

"Less than a day's ride," Niall mumbled.

Her eyes widened, and her chest heaved as if the mountain were sitting on it. That close? How was that possible? She'd walked endlessly after leaving Romeo. And she'd ridden more than a day.

Niall frowned. "Jamie dinna tell ye?"

"She dinna need to ken." At Jamie's sharp retort, Niall clamped his mouth shut. Voice muted; Jamie aimed an apologetic half-shrug at her. "Ye probably doubled back on yerself. I dinna want ye to worry."

All the confused emotions of the day bubbled up, and Sarah rose, her chair scraping loudly. "Worry?" Her eyes narrowed, and she mimicked the brogue. "Ye dinna want me to worry?" Her chest heaved, hands on her hips. She no longer cared if her breasts popped out of the top of her gown. "I suppose that's why you didn't tell me they held a knife to Rory. Or that they slaughtered Romeo and the family I left him with. So I wouldn't worry."

She'd said nothing, not wanting him to see how the guilt bothered her, how afraid she was, that she wanted to crawl into a hole and hide. Except she wasn't brave enough to, not without a ghost to comfort her.

Her eyes scanned the group. Wide-eyed with surprise, they gaped at her like the mad woman she probably was.

"And that's why you haven't told them who I am, isn't it? Because you didn't want me to worry about how they'd react? You don't think I'm smart enough to figure out my uncle probably destroyed the MacGorans? And that your men would slit my throat if they learned who I am?" Her voice broke, and she choked off a sob. "I know they call him the Devil of the Highlands. That I'm the spawn of the Devil. Why do you think I kept it from *you* for so long?"

The shocked silence beat at her. Horrified, they stared, frozen in place. Except for Jamie. Eyes clenched, jaw tight, he still didn't look at her. Hadn't since the night before, when she'd begged him to kiss her, then used his weakness against him when he objected. He'd said no, but she'd badgered him, touching him when he told her to stop. She'd made him swell up, and even asked him to tup her, and still he hadn't. Because he didn't want her.

How could she have been so stupid?

Her chair banged back and toppled into the shelving. In a haze of tears, she hurtled toward the door. A hand snagged her wrist as she rushed past, but she tore it away. In her haste, her skirt caught. The ripping split the silence, and pain wrenched through her knee. Still she ran, her hands banging against stone walls, knee exploding in agony as she stumbled up a flight of stairs. Up, up, up, she climbed. Around and around, the truth chased her until, finally, there was nowhere to go. Trapped in the tower room, she whirled and finally faced the truth.

She'd fallen in love with a man who couldn't bear the sight of her.

****

Jamie scowled as he slipped through the narrow opening into the cavern that night. The fire had died to mere embers and a chill filled the air. Most of the men had bedded down in the hall hours earlier while he and Malcolm discussed possible ways to penetrate Mitchell's castle. His head hurt as if he'd pounded it against the thick black walls. Sarah's outburst had caused an additional flood of questions he'd had to answer. All while she sulked in the tower.

For sulking was the only word that made sense.

A sliver of guilt shot through him as he glanced at her. Her diminutive form lay on the other side of the dying fire, a pile of blankets curled in shadow. Did she not realize how stunning she looked in her new finery? Carson swore it was his fault, that he'd hurt her feelings by not saying anything. But that was nonsense. Wasn't it? He'd shown her how much he wanted her the previous night. He shouldn't need to tell her.

As he turned to head for the basin of water to clean up, he tripped and banged into the wall. A cry arose, and he frowned. Another small bunch of plaid huddled beneath his feet.

"Rory? What are you doing in here?"

"Sarah asked me to. Tis all right, tis it not?" The boy rubbed at his sleepy eyes. "Sides, the snoring kept me awake last night."

"Tis fine." With a scratch at his neck, he eyed the sleeping figure across the room. Had she asked because she didn't want to be alone or for another reason?

He trudged to the basin and splashed water on his face then tossed another two logs onto the fire. As quietly as possible, he prepared for bed, then sank to the hard ground behind Sarah.

The bundled figure scooted away. He shimmied closer. Sarah edged nearer the growing flames, further from him.

He frowned. "Sarah? What are ye doing?"

"Nothing."

His head cocked, and a quiver of doubt niggled at him. Why was she even awake? "Come here, lass. Tis cold. Let me warm ye."

"No, thank you. I'm fine."

His eyes rolled, and a heavy sigh burst forth.

"Dinna be difficult. Tis nearly freezing." His arm snaked forward and hooked about her waist. She stiffened and pushed at his arm.

"Don't touch me."

The doubt hardened, and the iciness traveled into his chest. He didn't want to sleep alone. He liked waking to her curled around him. But he was too tired to play her games. "I'll not ask again, Sarah. Come here."

An unladylike harrumph busted up, but she said nothing. She merely pulled her blanket tighter around her shoulder.

The uneasy dread that had taken root during her outburst at dinner unfurled. Malcolm had suggested he might want to grovel as Bryan did when Jessica was upset, but that was ridiculous. He'd done nothing wrong, and Sarah wasn't breeding.

He latched onto the idea. She'd not had her monthly flow since she'd been with them. He'd seen perfectly sweet women turn into harridans beneath its force.

"Are ye bleeding, lass?" Hopeful, he lowered his voice so Rory wouldn't overhear. He'd ease it for her if she was cramping.

She flipped over, the sound of her body hitting the ground hard enough to make him wince. He didn't need to see her face. Her voice was as sharp as a glare. "No, I'm not bleeding. I just don't wish to be touched. I know you find that hard to believe, but it's the truth." Her hands popped out of the plaid and waved before her. "See? No hair twirling. Because I'm not lying."

She flipped back. Jamie stared at her, stunned.

He'd never been rejected. Not once in his twenty-seven years. With his sandy hair and greenish eyes, his looks alone attracted women of any age. Add his voice and the manners of a gentleman, and he'd never had to pay for company. He just showed interest, and they fell into his lap.

"I'll not beg, Sarah."

"Good. Because it will do you no good."

Defeated, Jamie let his head drop. The fire crackled, a sound easily mistaken for a witch cackling, and shadows cavorted in the darkness.

What had happened? And how could he fix it?

Chapter Thirteen

Sarah spent the next day in the tower where time seemed to have stopped. A massive carved chair bolted to the wall revealed remnants of a grand tapestry in its locked chest seat. It had required all of Malcolm's heft to break the lock. Faded and half finished, the fabric depicted a brilliantly colored scene of a knight and his maiden. Dark haired, the knight's features resembled Jamie's, with a strong jaw and penetrating eyes. The maiden glowed, her face lifted in adoration at the mounted champion, with hair the color of sunlight and brilliant sapphire eyes. Long and straight, her flaxen locks reached well beyond her waist, and her lips curled with the same merriment as Jamie's.

Draped across the seat, the cloth mocked her. The two figures looked madly in love, as if the world could never come between them. But if that were true, the song trapped in her head wouldn't exist. Like her journey up the stairs, the tune played over and over, an endless cycle of sorrow.

"May I join ye?"

Sarah turned away from the window and attempted a smile. Niall's arrival was the fifth in a seemingly endless stream. The whole morning, Jamie's men had popped in and out, starting with Malcolm's heroic effort to break into the chest. Shortly after, Jock had pressed her to finish off the excess scones from breakfast, luring her with a generous helping of precious honey. Logan had also breezed in to ask if she'd help dry some herbs he'd gathered, and she now had a rack of fragrant chives and nettle tied above her head.

"I'm not very talkative, but if you'd like to sit, please do."

"We're all worried about ye."

"It's not necessary." She gazed out the window. The perch overlooked the gardens and an increasingly large expanse of meadow destined for cattle and sheep grazing. Logan and one of Bryan's men toiled in the dirt, sowing seeds in neat little rows. On the edges of the clearing stood three figures, too distant to identify. She knew Jamie wasn't among them. He and Carson were scouting Mitchell Castle again, Jock had told her. Jamie, himself, continued to avoid her.

Had she made a mistake last night? Should she have accepted his offer to keep her warm?

In the light of day, she suspected she'd overreacted. He had every right to be angry. She'd blurted out the one thing he'd asked her to keep secret. Merely because she'd imagined he might have feelings for her.

"I'm a good listener, if ye'd like to talk."

Sarah leaned her head against the smooth arch of the arrow slit window. Lady Aalis had likely worn the small pocket into the embrasure as she stared out on the same view. Had she had a confidant? If she had, would she have made the same mistakes?

"I don't think I can," she admitted with a sigh. "It's all a jumble. None of it makes any sense."

Niall pushed himself away from the door frame

and circled the room. His fingers trailed the curve of the wall, his lightly tanned face lined with worry, until he reached her. Hesitantly, he reached for her hand.

She let him, but the touch left her unmoved. Not an unattractive man, with chocolate eyes and medium brown hair, he tended to blend into the background. Pleasant and reasonably learned, he spoke well and smiled easily, yet when he touched her or looked at her, it did nothing.

His thumb stroked the back of her knuckles.

"Have ye fallen in love with him then?"

"Jamie?" Well aware that's who he meant, she asked anyway, because saying his name made her feel more alive. Niall's worried brow robbed her of any comfort though. "No. Of course not. I barely know him."

Why she lied, she didn't know, any more than she understood why the Lost Lament haunted her every thought.

Niall's gaze flickered over her other hand, and she realized she'd been reaching for her hair. She scratched her neck instead.

"Ye would not be the first," he told her, his gaze following her hand. "And I hope ye haven't." He looked away and began to pace. Leather boots slapped against the stone floor; the rhythm oddly reminiscent of the tune in her head.

"He doesna mean to do it," he continued, voice laden with regret. "But he canna help himself. Women canna resist his charm, and he canna bear to hurt them. Never could. Even Joan. I dinna think he really loved her. But she wanted him, so he took her. Twas just as well she died. He would have hurt her eventually, or

138

they would have ended up hating each other."

"Do you think so?" Her own impression had been different. Jamie had sounded as if he loved Joan completely. But then, she'd imagined he had feelings for her as well.

Niall's face softened and his cheeks rounded. "I dinna ken them well. Just the few times he came to sing for the MacGregor. But Joan and my sister kenned each other as bairns so I had a number o' conversations with her. Joan was as ambitious as she was tiny. Twas part of why she wanted Jamie. She dreamed of being at court with Jamie as the King's bard."

Niall paused to trace the lines of the maiden's hair on the tapestry. "He would have been, too, had he wanted it. The Campbell was to be his step up. She nagged him something fierce when the Campbell showed interest. But he dinna really wish it. He only agreed in order to make her happy."

Niall glanced up as if afraid she'd stopped listening. She sent an encouraging half-smile, and he shrugged. "Doesna matter anymore. When she died, he changed. He lost his focus and started womanizing. Twasn't his fault. They threw themselves at him as often as not. And he always convinced himself he loved them. My sister was one of them. He courted her for a good year, but as soon as she started talking of weddings and bairns, he ended it. I canna say I was sorry. As much as I admire him, he isna a family man. Brianna ended up with a nice solid fellow. Has five little ones now."

A pang of longing ran through her. What would it be like, having babies? She had no idea, but the thought she would never have Jamie's left an empty pit in her stomach, like the day she had sent her friends away.

When she looked back, Niall's gaze never wavered. "Dinna let him hurt ye. I canna bear it if ye do."

He loves you. Don't doubt it.

The voice echoed in her head along with the melody, but Sarah wasn't sure who the voice meant, Niall or Jamie.

When she didn't answer, Niall crossed and took her hands in his. Earnest, his sable eyes held hers as tightly as his hands held her fluttering fingers. "Just say the word, Sarah, and I'll take ye away. I can protect ye. I'll take ye to your uncle or anywhere else ye want to go. All ye must do is ask."

"I can't." The thought unsettled her.

"Ye can. Twould be easy."

A chill breeze stirred the air, and she shivered. A sad knowing look crossed Niall's face, and he shrugged.

"I dinna think ye would, but if ye change yer mind…just ask."

A moment later, his boots pounded on the steps. Behind him, the haunting melody ceased, and Sarah found herself alone once more.

Chapter Fourteen

"Sarah? Sarah!"

Startled, Sarah's head snapped up, then froze. Was that Rory? She'd come downstairs for dinner and now sat with yet another pile of mending while the Highlanders trickled in. Wet from the incoming storm, they muttered and created the usual din, hanging their plaids before the fire while Jock groused at them and thunder rumbled in the distance. None of them seemed to hear the high pitched yell, though, so she lowered her gaze and slipped her needle into the newest victim of their rough existence.

Seconds later, Rory burst in, feet flying behind him.

"Come on, Sarah! We have to go! Hurry!"

He grabbed her hand and yanked. Around her, the commotion stalled. Heart stuttering, she bounded up, but her legs refused to cooperate. The folds of her skirt tangled, tripping her. Pain stabbed her thumb, and she stared as a drop of blood formed.

Rory tugged, eyes round with terror. "Hurry."

Finally, her feet moved. They raced toward the yawning black of the cavern. Stumbling, her leg wrenched, but she didn't dare slow. Behind her, voices yelled, then the shelf scraped and banged.

She gripped Rory's hand, fearing he'd pull her arm from the socket. Head spinning, he looked at the different choices of tunnels, then hurried toward the left one. She tumbled after him, unquestioning. No idea where they were headed, she followed, as blinded by fear as by the unrelenting dark.

Deeper and deeper they ran. When her lungs threatened to burst, Rory stopped, mumbling, then bolted toward another tunnel. Gasping, she hurtled forward. Left. Right. Straight ahead, then back to the right. A bolt of lightning beckoned them forward. They followed. Moments later, Rory slid to a stop.

Sarah nearly crashed into him. Bent forward at the waist, Rory stared, gasping. Icy pellets bruised their faces as they stared into unending darkness.

Another streak of lightning highlighted the view. Black water churned below, a frothing hungry maw. Torrents of rain slammed their forms.

"We…" He gasped. "…have… to go." He pointed.

Too dark to see, she heard the water cascading down the steep incline. Rocky and narrow, the path twisted, sharp corners doubling back when the ground dropped off unexpectedly. She'd barely managed it with Jamie's help. Now Rory wanted her to do it in a dress? In the middle of a storm? In the dark?

"Why?" Her gaze whisked about, but there was nothing to see.

"They know."

"Who?" Her breath hitched. He didn't answer, didn't need to. "How?"

His hand tugged, then let go. In the pitch dark, she reached for his form. Tremors ran up her arm. He was as scared as she.

"Why can't I hide in the tunnels?" She looked back at the marginally darker blackness behind her, then clutched her skirt. With shaking fingers, she bunched it up and knotted it above her knees.

"They know."

Her last hope died. She peered at the path, a mere memory directing her. Even if they clambered down, where would they go?

"Lady Aalis told me." The words came from further away. "There's a place you can hide. But we have to hurry."

Gingerly, Sarah followed his voice. Stones slipped and water splashed with each step. Throat in her mouth the whole way, she clutched at bare roots and slick stems. Her fingers bled, rocks scraping the tender flesh, the blood washed away by icy water. Through it all, she wished for Jamie.

Finally, she caught up to Rory, his labored breath halting her.

"Ye aren't going to like it, Sarah." Her stomach tightened. Now that her eyes had adjusted to the dark, she saw his arm point.

A darker slit in the rock, the hole looked smaller than her father's coffin. Tucked beneath a clump of bushes and a rock overhang, the space was as enticing as death.

"I can't." She backed away. Her foot slipped.

Rory grabbed her.

Beneath her, the loch roared, black and writhing.

"Please, Sarah. There's not much time."

"I can't. It's too small." Too dark. Too tight. Too lonely.

Too nervous to stay still, Rory hopped, spraying water and rocks. "You have to. They'll kill us all if they find ye."

"They will anyway."

"Nay. They'll wait, hoping we'll lead them to ye."

Lightning streaked overhead. Sarah jumped. A second later, the sky rumbled and cracked.

Petrified, she stared at the black maw.

From above, shouts rang out, magnified by the tunnel.

"All right." Hands fisted, she tried to move but couldn't.

"Sarah!" The bellow spewed from the darkness. Euanan.

She dropped to her knees. Gravel shredded her sodden skirt. She scrambled forward, pushed by the driving rain.

With a silent prayer, she wedged herself into the opening. Cold, wet earth pinched her lungs, squeezing the breath from her. Dirt showered her head, threatening to bury her, but she shimmied herself around and tucked her legs up, knees under her chin. If they found her, she'd die facing them. If possible, she'd push them off the path and cheer as the pond swallowed them.

Rory thrust a knife at her.

"Stab them in the eyes." As tiny as she was, he shoved her back and jammed her into the mud. Wool flapped in the wind, nearly sailing away as he stripped the plaid from his shoulders, revealing the light of his shirt. He rammed the kilt toward her, sticking the edges between her and the rapidly crumbling ground.

"This will hide ye a bit." The weight of the wool pressed down, thick and confining. Then he began to tear at the earth above her. Frantic, he kept peering up, over his shoulder. The shouts grew louder.

The lump in Sarah's throat swelled. Sharp stones jabbed at her eyelids. Roots snaked into the crack between her lips. She clenched her teeth, dirt crunching.

It would never work!

Frantic, her body began to shake.

Easy, child.

Her head jerked back. Then the gentle croon of the Lost Lament drifted through her mind.

Lady Aalis?

I'm here.

The rapid suck of Sarah's breath slowed. Overhead, the constant rumble of thunder eased. Rory's hands patted at the plaid, rubbing dirt over the porous surface.

"We'll be back for ye."

Terrified, Sarah listened for more, but there was nothing else. He was gone.

She was alone. Again.

She wanted to scream, but her throat was too tight.

Breathe, Sarah. Jamie needs you.

A sob bubbled up, and tears pricked her eyes. She hugged her knees.

She couldn't do this. It was too hard.

You can. You're a Clinton and a Campbell. You're strong.

Water trilled along her hairline, just as her father's fingers used to do. Her chin trembled.

Relax. Try to sleep.

She snorted. A moist, loamy scent filled her nose. But the haunting melody swirled through her head and calmed her. She concentrated on it, taking slow even breaths until the song filled her.

Slowly, the cold enveloped her. As she shivered,

the dirt began to shift, creeping around her, but she pushed the fear back. She'd done it before. How many times had Eilidh shut her away, leaving her for days? Why would God have allowed it if not to prepare her for this? She had to do this. For Jamie.

He'd warm her up. Later.

After a while, the shivering stopped. Her head fell forward. From far away, she heard the storm ease. Shouts broke out, and she heard men skid past. Too cold to care, she slipped away, into the endless dark, her breathing slowing and slowing and slowing.

****

They froze when someone hammered at the front door. They'd come in from their chores when the black clouds began to roll in, and Rory had charged through seconds before, so they were ready, but still it sent a shudder through Jamie.

"MacIan? Ye in there?" The voice echoed through the hall and into the kitchen. Another round of thumping jarred their ears.

A quick glance around mirrored Jamie's reaction. Niall's ruddy complexion paled, and Rob and Logan reached for their dirks. Jamie shook his head while his own fingers clenched. With six men patrolling, no one should have arrived unannounced.

"Aye." Normally deep, it came out raspy, so Jamie cleared his throat and shouted. "Who's there?" He didn't need to ask. A dread had been building the entire evening. He'd attributed it to Sarah's continued aloofness, but Rory's frantic yell had solidified it.

A quick glance toward the shelving unit allowed him to inhale. Jock had closed it. The pots and pans clanged into place. A quick swipe of his leg obliterated the mark on the floor.

"Tis Euanan Mitchell. I implore ye to shelter us from the storm."

A gesture sent Irving toward the door as Jamie arched his brows. The Euanan he knew never implored. One season at Mitchell Castle had taught Jamie enough about both men that he'd never returned. He hadn't enjoyed playing the music Hammond had requested, and the coin had been meager. But watching Euanan lord it over men with more intelligence and brawn, merely because he was Hammond's son, had left a distaste in his mouth.

With as confident a stride as possible, Jamie led his men into the great hall. Too large and difficult to heat due to a gaping hole in the ceiling, they rarely congregated there, but the expansive arches afforded more room to swing a sword than the kitchen. He'd not fight if it could be avoided, but if it was inevitable, he'd be prepared.

At Jamie's curt nod, Irving lifted a thick timber from the double door. The doors spewed open, disgorging eight sodden hulks. Like deformed English Sheepdogs clad in black and blue tartan, they burst into the room. Water sprayed from bearded faces, and mud pooled at their feet.

Jamie's jaw clenched. At least it wasn't blood dribbling on Sarah's mopped floor.

Behind them, Euanan strolled in, a dark green cape swirling about his gentlemanly form. Unlike the others, he sported wide breeches of doeskin instead of a kilt and a large brimmed black hat. The water sluiced from him as if unwilling to impinge upon his cuffed boots.

How had they slipped by six of his men? Worry

settled, thick and gut-wrenching. There were eight here. One more than his men if you counted Euanan, each larger than everyone but Malcolm. But how many were outside?

A drop of water splatted on Jamie's neck. He reached up and swiped it away then peered at the ceiling. Another drop glistened, ready to ambush him. He stepped aside. His foot dragged a bucket into place. He'd count the drops as they fell to keep him from thinking about Sarah and how scared she had to be.

"Euanan." He nodded.

"Sorry to barge in, uninvited," Euanan said. He shrugged his cape off and surveyed the room. In a flash, his eyes examined the huge fireplace, with the dusty pot hook and cobwebs in the corners, then circled over the huge beams in the ceiling. His lips curled with disgust at the hole above Jamie. "Do you mind if we start a fire? I doubt we can fit in the kitchen with you." He picked his way around the puddles to peer into the kitchen and threw his cape over a vacant chair. "Ye needn't feed us. We won't be here that long."

Splat.

"How long *do* ye intend to be here?" Jamie shot a questioning look at Malcolm. A nearly imperceptible movement of his chin confirmed Jaime's assessment. They couldn't fight their way out. Not with any guarantee of success.

"As long as it takes."

With a flick of his wrist, Euanan signaled his men. One of them pulled the door open. Jamie's hand tightened around his dirk as three more men dragged Drew, Ramsay, and Ned into the room. Half conscious, Drew's head lolled against his chest, blood dripping from his temple. Ned struggled against a man three times larger, arms pinned behind him. Nose broken, red streamed around a lump on his chin. Ramsay appeared unhurt, aside from a small slit in his upper left arm. He clutched his right wrist though, face white with pain, while a burly man nudged him forward at the point of a blade.

Spat… splat… ping. Four, Jamie counted as another chill raced down his spine.

"I'm afraid three others put up too much of a fight." Euanan's head shook, a false expression of regret lining his fair face. "If they aren't dead, they will be soon. Tis too cold out there to last long."

The pit in Jamie's stomach churned. Three dead already? How many more before they left?

A fifth drop smacked into the bucket. Thunder rumbled, closer. He shuddered. Was this his curse? To relive the same nightmare over and over?

His gaze wandered over his men. One by one, they returned it. Even Ramsay, who hated the Campbells, nodded, one curt bob of his head. Whatever his feelings toward her clansmen, Ramsay would fight, and even die, to protect Sarah.

"Will ye kill us all, Euanan? To retrieve a lass we dinna have?"

"Nay." Euanan shrugged, then sent a silent command with his eyes. "We've no quarrel with you or the MacGregor."

No quarrel, and yet they had killed three and held a bare blade against Ned's exposed throat.

"Give up your weapons and let us search until the storm passes. Once I'm sure she's not here, we'll leave."

Euanan's gaze flitted over Jamie's men while, one by one, Euanan's henchmen disarmed them. Even the small stiletto blades hidden in their boots were plucked away and tossed into a pile in the corner. When Robert growled in protest, Jamie's sharp command stopped him. He refused to lose anyone in a futile battle.

"Where's the lad?" Euanan asked as the last weapon clattered atop the pile. "I know ye've two men watching Mitchell Castle, and everyone else is here or dead. She'll not escape alone. She's too simple."

When no one answered, Euanan turned on his heel and marched into the kitchen. His boots thudded, and Jamie's throat tightened. Euanan lifted an arm and pointed. With a single heave, the shelf crashed to the floor and splintered into three pieces.

Another drip, the eighth, plunked. His stomach lurched, and lightning flashed through the hole.

Had Ramsay betrayed them?

No, it wasn't Ramsay. His bloodless face went whiter, and his eyes stared at the cavern opening, wide with disbelief.

Euanan's laugh crawled up Jamie's spine. "Did ye think no one would betray ye?" As the laugh rolled over them, men began to emerge from the caverns. Not only had they learned the way in, they had found the exits, too. Or been shown them.

Jamie turned an anguished look on his men. If not Ramsay, then who? Who had a reason?

"I'd execute him for ye, but tis more fun to let ye wonder."

Duff, the man who'd led the first search, spurted from the tunnel with a grin splitting his face. "She was here."

His fist rose, then released the stranglehold he had on the tattered silk Sarah had worn when she arrived. It fluttered to bunch at Euanan's feet. "There's three exits. I stationed men at each one."

The sliver of hope Jamie held shattered, then reformed. They knew, but they hadn't found her. Or Rory.

Another drop slithered along his spine. Twelve.

Euanan's face twisted. He stomped into the hole, crouching to fit. Voices filtered back out, angry words that peppered the silence until a bellow rose a few minutes later. "Sarah!"

The tension in Jamie's shoulders eased a tad. His men grumbled and cursed but Euanan's men poked and prodded them into submission. The enemy swarmed over every inch of the ruins, shattering chests and breaking chairs.

Throughout, the water kept dripping. Plop... plop... plop, like hesitant heartbeats, a tortuous reminder.

He'd failed. Again. He'd promised Sarah protection, and he'd failed. He'd put his men in danger. Rory was in danger, again. Why?

Because he'd refused help. The price had been too high.

Would it be so bad, pledging his allegiance? Bryan hadn't asked for it. It was his own sense of honor that had doomed them.

Where was Sarah? Had Rory hidden her somewhere? Was Rory with her? Or was she alone?

When Euanan exited the cavern a few minutes later, his face twisted into a snarl. Eyes burning with anger, he scrutinized each of Jamie's men before jabbing his dirk in Robert's direction.

Two men jerked Robert to his knees, head ripped back, and Euanan's knife hovered near his eye.

"Where is she?" Euanan demanded.

Robert glowered back, betraying his nonchalant shrug. "I've only been here a few days. But even if I did ken, I'd not tell ye."

"Not even if you'll die?" Euanan edged closer and lowered the blade until it nicked Robert's jugular.

Robert snorted. "I've faced death for less." His eyes narrowed, turning black. "And the MacGregor will avenge me. Twill cost you two men for every one ye kill today."

Jamie saw Euanan hesitate. The blade trembled, but then it jammed forward with a sickening sucking noise. Jaw clenched with barely controlled rage, Euanan twisted the blade. Robert's eyes widened. Jamie closed his eyes. Air gurgled, mixed with the metallic scent of blood. Robert slumped.

Another drop of water splattered.

The door banged. Drenched, a man rushed in and whispered to Euanan, hands flapping. Euanan swallowed, his grip on the bloody dirk clenched, and his eyes grew fevered.

He spun, flailing the dirk at Niall, then Jock, then Malcolm. None flinched. Malcolm's lips curled in a scornful grin, and Jock spit at his feet.

"Will you watch them all die?" he screamed as he rounded on Jamie. "For a girl? A weak, crippled, pathetic Sassenach?"

Jamie lifted his chin. "Why do ye want her if she's so distasteful? Is it because she rejected ye?" When Euanan blinked and his nostrils flared, Jamie continued,

"Nay? Must be your da then. Did he threaten to disown ye? *Again*. If ye dinna bring her back?"

The slack mouthed gape was a small victory and short-lived. Euanan recovered. His neck snaked back, then he leaned into Jamie's face. A foul stench spewed forth.

"Da liked your wife, you ken?" Jamie stiffened. "Especially when she screamed. He told me about it. She screamed your name, over and over, while he enjoyed her." Euanan's laugh was brittle. "And all these years you thought it was the Campbells."

Stunned, Jamie ground his teeth. Water battered at his neck. Euanan's mouth curved up, in a smug smile. Then pain stabbed at Jamie's waist. He glanced at the red stain growing over his shirt. His palm settled over the wound. When he lifted it, watery blood dripped from his fingers.

"Ye fecking bastard." Jock launched himself. Before he reached Euanan, a fist slammed into his head, and he crumpled to the ground with a sickening thud.

"I'm done here." Euanan strolled toward his cape, swirled it around him, then headed toward the door. Numb, Jamie just watched. The door swung wide. Three more monsters tromped through the door.

A small, limp form hurtled through the air and hit the floor with a mewling cry. Watery pink oozed from it.

"There's your brat. We found him in the bushes." Euanan and his men shuffled out, weapons waving. "He hid her. Even admitted it." Euanan's eyes wandered up toward the black maw in the ceiling. "Hope he tells you where. Before he dies. She won't last long."

****

The dread tightened like a wet leather strap tied around a swollen foot.

Dazed, it took Jamie a moment to move. By the time he did, Malcolm had Rory cradled in his arms and Jock was coming to, a lump forming next to his right eye.

"Ye all right, Jamie?" Malcolm shouldered past to lay Rory on the stone hearth while Jamie peered at the hole in his side. Aside from the warm blood, the wound was a minor distraction.

Was he all right? He wasn't sure. Blood trickled between his fingers, and Euanan's words rang in his head. But neither mattered.

Another drop of water exploded. He gazed at the wet darkness above.

"We have to find Sarah." His eyes locked on Rory, his broken body covered in mud and blood. He rushed forward, heart pumping in beats as slow as the drops falling from the ceiling.

Rory jerked away from Jamie's touch. Two jagged bones stuck out from the left arm, and a slice on the right ran from elbow to wrist. Blood welled on the worn hearth, congealing into a shiny black and red mess. One of Rory's legs bent at a strange angle. As soon as Jamie pulled his hand away, the boy's head fell back, a serene look whitening his face. Jamie recognized the look; he'd seen it too many times.

"Ack, Rory boy." The endearment fell from his lips while tears formed in his eyes. He smoothed the wet curls back. Through how many childhood fevers and nightmares had he comforted Rory? How many times had the imp run in and woke him, excited by some everyday event? Who would fill the silence if not Rory?

"I...dinna tell." As quiet as a whisper, Jamie heard the words as he dropped his head. His heart cleaved in two, the pain as extreme as it had been when he found his own child dead.

No, it hurt more. They'd never even named his boy. Joan had liked none of his choices, and he'd been unwilling to accept hers. He'd mourned an idea. This time he'd mourn an actual soul.

Jamie lifted his head and stemmed the tears. He mustered a sad smile and stroked Rory's cheek. "Ye did well, lad. Better than I could have."

"Tis cold." Rory's arm convulsed. His face twisted. Heat blazed behind him, fed by a log Irving threw on the neglected fire, but it wasn't enough to warm Rory. Nothing was.

"I ken." A blanket dropped over Rory, a familiar blue and green plaid. They'd bury him in it.

Rory's eyes scrunched closed. "Nay...Sarah." He forced his eyes open, his head turning toward Jamie. "My...gift." Pink bubbled between his chalky lips. His eyes started to roll back in his head, then his lips curved up in the corners. "Mam's waiting," he breathed.

Jamie held his own breath, hoping, but another breath never came from the small lungs. A quiet plop of water made him wince before the dam of tears burst. Shoulders heaving, he buried his face in his arms.

They'd taken everything from him. He'd thought the Campbells responsible. But it had been Hammond Mitchell. And now they'd taken Rory, too.

His head lifted, and he sucked in a lungful of the metallic scent of blood.

They wouldn't get Sarah.

He lumbered to his feet and directed his gaze at the

remainder of his men. They stared at Rory as if they expected him to jump up and proclaim it a sick joke. Tears streaked Jock's ruddy cheeks, and Malcolm's huge form looked ready to crumble.

"We mourn later." Hoarse and broken, Jamie forced the words out. "After we find Sarah."

"We've no idea where to look," Drew protested. "What makes ye think we can find her? They couldn't." He thumbed his fist at the door.

"We look anyway." Jamie turned toward the battered bits of wood that had failed to shield her. "Besides, Rory told us." He offered up a silent thanks. "She's somewhere near the pond."

Niall and Logan's eyes widened as the reference to the day she'd bathed registered. Jamie squeezed Jock's shoulder and told him to stay with Rory, but Jock wrenched himself away. Within minutes, every one of them streamed out into the icy rain.

The first of Euanan's remaining men died without a sound. Stationed a few feet from the entrance, the scout never heard them. Drew retrieved his dirk from the man's left eye as they cascaded around the body. The next screamed, his cry swallowed by drizzle as Malcolm crushed his windpipe. At Jamie's curt command, Logan and Alastair chewed their way along the path to take out any others while Ramsay and Niall ignited torches.

Soon, six lights flickered the length of the thin, rocky passage.

How long did she have? Jamie's neck and shoulders ached as he peered at the rocks and bushes. He'd counted the drops of water as they toppled. At first, it had been to calm himself, but every drop annoyed him more. Each was another space of time, another instant not knowing where she was, another heartbeat of uncertainty and helplessness. Now the rain beat at him, faster and colder, reminding him that time was rapidly expiring.

It had been twenty minutes already, at least. It only took ten to fifteen for a body to lose consciousness in these conditions. He'd seen hardened men die in as little as half an hour. Which was exactly what Euanan had been taunting him with, talking of the cold and rain. At most, she had an hour, assuming Rory had tucked her somewhere out of the elements.

But where? He'd never seen any other caverns or crevasses along the path.

"Down here!"

The hope in Ramsay's voice galvanized him. Jamie's feet slipped and floundered as he careened toward the unknown, toward the five coalescing points of light.

He lurched to a stop before colliding with Malcolm. Drew and Ramsay kneeled at a bend in the path, shoveling rocks and dirt with their hands, while the others looked on, tapers held high. Heart in his throat, Jamie dropped to his knees. His torch sputtered as it hit the ground. Water ran in rivulets, gurgling as it rushed past, the corners of a cloth struggling to escape the torrent.

"God's teeth," Ramsay swore as he tore the fabric away. Mud sprayed like tiny shards of ice, slapping Jamie's cheek and neck.

Drew froze.

Ramsay muttered and fell back on his heels. "I... Shite!"

Jamie stared in disbelief. Scrunched up in what amounted to a hole the size of a small ale barrel, Sarah listed to the side, unresponsive.

"No." Choking, he staggered closer. Frantic, he swiped at the mud dripping over her pale face. Icy, her curls sliced at his knuckles, her skin as hard and lifeless as the ground beneath him.

Desperate, he pulled at her limbs and dragged her from the offensive space. The water on his cheeks grew warmer. Tears, not raindrops.

"She's dead, Jamie."

He threw Malcolm's hand off and wrapped her in his arms. "Nay." Lurching, he stumbled to his feet and cradled her against his chest. She couldn't be dead. He wouldn't allow it.

His lips touched her head. The smell of roots and decay filled his nostrils. He forced his feet to move, one after the other. Around him, the men fell back, steadying him when he faltered, saying nothing while he shuffled back up the incline toward the cavern entrance.

Please, Lady, I love her. Don't let her die not knowing.

As if in answer, the rain paused and the wind died. Not reassured, he forged onward until familiar black walls swallowed them. Jamie closed off his ears, unwilling to accept the muttering and the funereal sound of their footsteps echoing through the earth.

She wasn't dead. She couldn't be. God wouldn't be that unfair.

Even if she was dead, he'd not leave her. She'd never again be cold and alone. He'd hold her and warm her. If God existed, He'd bring her back. She didn't deserve to die. Tales of less worthy men who'd returned from the dead echoed through his mind. He'd never believed them, thought they were allegories or metaphors, but if there was even a chance they were real…

Exhausted, Jamie fell to his knees when he reached the cavern. He couldn't take her into the kitchen. Not with Rory's body there.

Gently, he laid her on the ground and stripped the plaids from their bodies, hers sodden and covered in wet earth. Wordlessly, Malcolm understood, and soon a fire blazed in the middle of the cave. The others hovered until Jamie barked at them, then they shuffled out, murmuring and muttering.

Holding back tears, he sliced Sarah's remaining garments away, then dried her with the lambswool Malcolm handed him, his hands caressing the curve of her elbow and the line of her arm. He stroked the water and mud from her, washing her with warm water, then drying her again. Meanwhile, he prayed fervent promises of faith he'd stopped uttering when Joan died, convinced that God didn't exist, but the words flowed from him with the power of hope. Not Catholic prayers, not Calvinistic invocations or Druidic promises of sacrifices, but heart-felt entreaties swearing eternal belief if just this once God answered him.

When Sarah's limp body gleamed as cleanly as possible, Jamie stripped then lifted her onto his lap. Atop a pile of dry tartans, he wrapped her in his arms and tugged yards of wool around them. Then he leaned back and stared at the flickering red flames.

"Come back to me, love," he whispered, voice raw, "or take me with ye."

Chapter Fifteen

Jamie had never been so numb with cold as when he jerked awake a short time later. His entire body shivered, despite a fire blasting in his face. He wasn't sure how long he'd slept, but his lips were scorched, and his throat was as parched as a dried kipper.

"Malcolm?" He winced at the croak and turned his head.

How could he still be so frigid? Malcolm had stripped to his braies and rivulets of sweat trailed his hairy chests in spades.

"Ye sound like ye need some water."

Jamie snaked an arm out of the blankets and accepted the tankard. Sarah still lay against him, a small unmoving bundle against his stomach and chest. Stiff, he rolled his shoulders and neck before draining the cup. Even the water was tepid, but he gulped it down.

He'd fallen asleep bargaining with God, but apparently, God wasn't listening. Sarah hadn't moved.

"How long?"

"An hour or so."

An hour. If she was coming back, she would have by now. Jamie's eyes pricked but were too dry for tears. He'd promised so many things he couldn't remember them all. Now, it didn't matter.

"Do we have any whiskey?" Maybe he could drink himself to death. Freezing wasn't working.

"Jamie?" Malcolm peered at him, brows dipping and inched closer. "Is that ye shivering or Sarah?"

Without waiting for an answer, Malcolm tore the blankets away. Heat blasted over them and Jamie realized he wasn't as cold as he'd thought.

Malcolm's lips stretched into a slow grin as his hand reached out to test Sarah's pulse. "I think she's alive."

Afraid to believe it, Jamie stared at Malcolm's ruddy hand. Against the pale, bluish cast of Sarah's skin, it looked huge and steady. Tiny quivers rippled her limbs and filled him like the notes of a sonnet.

Hands trembling, he hugged her. Tears leaked out the corner of his eyes. He swiped them away.

"Send for Bryan." His voice shook, as hoarse as if he'd not had the water. "We need more men. And I need his counsel. I canna do this alone. I was a fool to think I could." His pride had cost Rory his life as surely as Euanan had.

"He's already here." Malcolm threw the blankets back over them and stepped away. "I suspect that was what sent Euanan out of here without his prize. He's been at the MacDonalds' for near a week. Jessica, too."

Jamie frowned. "I thought Gus said she wouldn't let him come."

"Nay, he said she wouldn't let him leave her. Never said anything about not coming. Twas her that made him ride out last night when the MacDonald's scout noticed Mitchell's men slinking through the woods."

Jamie cocked his head. The cold had left him tired and achy, but apparently his brain was sluggish, too. As fierce a reputation as Bryan had, one man wasn't enough to scare Euanan away.

"Just Bryan?"

"Nay. Sixty men rode with him."

"Sixty?" Jamie snapped his mouth shut. With another sixty men, Euanan never would have dared step foot on his land. "Why?" He'd been less than a day away? For a week? With sixty men?

"Ye wanted to do this on yer own." As always, Malcolm had the answer. "Bryan knows that and wanted to respect it. He was waiting for ye to ask."

Jamie sank back. His hands stroked Sarah, savoring the fact she lived. Jessica had told him he was a fool before he left. She'd told him to take what Bryan had offered—thirty men and their families. But he'd wanted to prove himself. He didn't have enough to pay for the supplies needed. He wouldn't risk the women and children, even knowing that another thirty MacGregor warriors would have discouraged exactly what had happened.

But Bryan had told her to leave him alone, that it wasn't her business. It had always been Bryan's weakness, caring what others wanted. He hid it from his enemies, and even from most others, but his friends and Jessica understood it. Especially Jessica. She tempered it, pointing it out in no uncertain terms when he was an idiot.

Bryan was likely pacing the hall now, barking at everyone, afraid that Jamie would hate him for interfering.

"Get him in here," Jamie said. "We need to make plans."

****

Sarah's head pounded the next day as she sat by

the fire and listened to the three men argue.

She'd woke the day before for a short time to find Malcolm and Jamie conferring with a man nearly as big as Malcolm. With a fiery beard, a muscled chest, and a voice that rivaled Malcolm's in pitch, Bryan MacGregor was the most intimidating man she'd ever met.

Unlike Malcolm, he never smiled, except when he looked at his wife. She too flustered Sarah. Tall and stately, with flowing copper curls and soft brown eyes, Jessica was fearless. They'd done their best to be quiet. Sheltered by the plaids and the warmth of Jamie's heartbeat against her ear, she'd had no trouble falling back to sleep. Today was a different matter altogether.

"I'm telling ye, tis impenetrable," Jamie insisted for the umpteenth time. He sat at the table, fingers clutching the hair on either side of his head as they stared at the crudely drawn map. "I'll not ask ye to sacrifice men for a lost cause. We'll find another way." He looked exhausted, his tanned face darkened by shadows and a faint beard he'd not bothered to shave.

"Ye aren't asking. I'm telling. Just as I told ye to take my men before."

"You didn't tell him, dear." Jessica's hand stroked her husband's shoulder as she passed behind Bryan, pacing the room in long, unladylike strides while her other hand caressed her belly. "*I* told him. *You* asked." Sarah watched her circle the group, fascinated. At six months, her stomach jutted out before her, but she still moved with a grace Sarah envied.

"Aye." Bryan's face softened, sheepish, and his hand grabbed Jessica's until she passed. Mossy green eyes followed his wife with obvious adoration. A pang of jealousy shot through Sarah so sharp and deep she had to shut her eyes and ears.

Why could they have it and not her?

Jamie had told her he loved her last night. The thrill of joy had been nigh unbearable as had the agony that followed. He'd said it each time she woke, murmuring it in her ear, and kissed her back to sleep. Early, in the hours when the fire had burned to embers and she rested enough to stay awake for more than mere minutes, she'd kissed him back. As much as she tried, though, she'd been unable to echo the words.

He wanted to marry her, he'd said, and her heart had broken. The one thing she wanted more than life itself would cost him his.

Sarah's eyes wandered to the dip in the hearth. They'd moved Rory and scrubbed the hearth, but the dark stain remained. Her eyes ached with unshed tears.

"Dammit!" Bryan's fist slammed on the table. Sarah jumped. "There has to be a way. I'll not let the bastard win. He slaughtered my men."

"He'll not win." Jamie's voice was heavy with grief, and his eyes connected with hers. She sent him a sad smile. "But losing more men willna bring anyone back."

"Then he's won. If he doesna pay, he's won," Bryan said. He levered himself up from the table and joined his wife. In an opposite circle, he paced, green eyes glowing with frustrated rage, feet slamming the floor. Every step made Sarah's head pound harder.

"He'll not win. He'll not get Sarah. Alex is less than two days away, and Paddy said he's livid." Jamie's voice dripped with frustration.

"And without a way in, he'll not win either."

Malcolm shifted and rubbed the bridge of his nose.

Jamie's head fell forward. His hands gripped his head. "I ken."

Sarah bounded up, unable to listen to the same argument again. They had gone around and around the whole morning. Grabbing the simple woolen skirt Jessica had provided, she flew toward the door.

Jamie captured her wrist as she passed. "What's wrong, love?"

"Nothing," she lied. "I just need some quiet."

She wrenched her arm away to escape the same way she had the day after Jamie had touched her so intimately. Unlike that time, when her feet had been covered by nothing but strips of fabric, her borrowed leather shoes slapped the steps. Tears stung her eyes, and the heaviness of her heart made her think she'd never reach the top of the tower. When she did, she rushed to the window and dragged in great gulps of air.

It wasn't fair. Jamie loved her. She loved him. Why couldn't they have what the MacGregors had?

She stared out at the budding trees, as green as the eyes of Jamie's laird. The world was blossoming, hope springing forth. The MacGregor's men swarmed the rock-strewn courtyard. Shouts carried on the air, along with the music of life. Soon, the castle would be complete, and families would fill the rooms. Cottages would dot the landscape and sheep would roam the mountainside.

But she wouldn't be here to see it, just as Rory and Gus and two of the MacGregors men wouldn't. And the only way to ensure Jamie and the rest were here was to go back.

A fat tear burned her hand.

"Can I come in?"

The dulcet voice startled her, and she whirled. She swiped at the tear, too choked up to say she wanted to be alone.

Aside from a slight pant and one hand clutching her back, Jessica floated into the room as if she weren't pregnant. With a slight toss of her red hair, she hesitated in the doorway until Sarah nodded.

"It's quite the pickle, isn't it?" In a continuation of the pacing she'd left off below, Jessica circled the much smaller room in six steps.

Too polite to not reply, Sarah agreed with a heavy sigh.

Jessica slowed as she came around in front of Sarah, then her cheery countenance faded. "They don't understand, do they?"

"Understand what?"

Jessica pulled out a snowy white linen and offered it. Sarah took it and wiped her cheek. "What it's like to be a woman. To be bartered, and in some cases sold, for influence and money."

"No. No, I don't suppose they do." Sarah strangled the handkerchief, wishing it was Hammond or Euanan's neck instead of a simple piece of fabric. Then at least Jamie would get what he wanted and she wouldn't have to sacrifice herself.

"You don't think Alexander will let Jamie have you, do you? No matter what."

Her head whipped around in denial. That someone understood eased the ache, but not enough. "Jaime's not powerful enough. And I'm worth too much."

"Hmm. I thought as much. Jamie tends to overlook the value of money. To him, it's just a necessary evil.

That you can buy and sell the entire city of Glasgow would never enter his mind." Jessica paused her latest circle to glance back over her shoulder. "You *are* that Clinton family, aren't you?"

"Yes." She'd never before considered it a disadvantage. Now, though, she'd give anything to be the nobody Eilidh had claimed.

Silence descended, aside from the rustle of Jessica's skirt as she continued her rounds. A small dirk appeared. Long fingers flipped the blade while she chewed her bottom lip, lost in thought.

Disheartened, Sarah twisted her head to gaze out the tower window. A light breeze tickled her neck, and a warbling coo called to her. Leaning out, she spotted a plump rock woodcock. Its head bobbed as it strutted on a thin outcropping. As she watched, another flew in and deposited a bit of straw. The first took the offering and added it to a pile.

Soon, the nest would be full with tiny hungry mouths. A pang of loss settled in her heart.

"May I ask something, Jessica?"

"Of course. Anything."

"What does it feel like? To make love?"

The question halted Jessica's pacing. Her knife stopped twirling, and she frowned.

"I'm sorry. I shouldn't have asked." Sarah spun back around and stared at the birds. "It's just that I'll never know. And I wondered."

"Oh, dear." An awkward pause followed, then Jessica shuffled over and laid a tentative hand on Sarah's shoulder. "I'm sorry. I assumed..." Her dulcet tones trailed off, then resumed, "Though it shouldn't surprise me now that I think about it."

The hand withdrew, leaving Sarah lonely, but she lifted her chin. "He said he wouldn't. That my husband would expect a virgin, and he couldn't risk it."

Jessica snorted. "Men are fools, and no one but Jamie would even worry about it. It isn't as if women haven't fooled their grooms for centuries."

"What do you mean?" Sarah turned and cocked her head.

Jessica shrugged, a movement that reminded Sarah of Malcolm's. "Men make love. Most fall asleep practically before they're done. All it takes is a tiny smear of blood and the most experienced woman in the world is an instant virgin."

The look on her face must have betrayed her confusion because Jessica's head went back. "Oh, dear. Jamie said you were innocent. I didn't realize." She grasped Sarah's hands after tossing away the twisted handkerchief. "You have no idea, do you? Is that why you asked?"

Sarah glanced at the nesting doves. "Jamie tried to explain some of it. And I think I've guessed at a lot of it. But I want to know. I want to experience it. With someone I choose, not someone who's chosen for me." She didn't add that she only had one night to accomplish it.

A slow, impish smile lit Jessica's face, and she squeezed Sarah's hands. "Honey, I can definitely help you with that. Some men are difficult, but not the three downstairs. It's easy to get them to do anything."

"It is?"

Jessica's laughter trilled. "Of course. Just cry. It works every time. With Jamie and Bryan, anyway. Malcolm's a little harder. Come, sit down, and we'll talk."

****

A full moon rode in the sky by the time the men gave up for the night. Sarah waited, clad in the gossamer lace nightgown Jessica had loaned her, until Jamie's tired steps climbed the stairs. Around the room, a small fire burned in the hearth and candles dotted the space. After they talked, Jessica had suggested she sprinkle lavender about the room, so a delicate floral scent drifted through the air. Why, she wasn't sure, but after she recounted her ill-conceived attempt to mop the floor, Jessica had declared it essential.

As the steps grew closer, Sarah wiped her hands on her hips and inhaled. She felt more naked in the nightgown than if she'd worn nothing. Positioned so the moonlight framed her from behind, there was no way Jamie could resist her. Or so Jessica had said.

Jamie paused, one foot on the top step. His quick intake of breath confirmed Jessica's theory. As did the spark in his eyes.

"What are ye wearing?" He swallowed, and his gaze burned along her breasts. She flushed, and her nipples tightened against the brush of lace.

"Do you like it? Jessica loaned it to me." Uncertain, she hid her hands behind her back to prevent them wringing.

He didn't look aroused as much as angry. The angle of his jaw hardened, and a scowl formed on his brow. His brows lowered further as his gaze wandered below her waist. "Tis very pretty."

Jamie averted his eyes and moved into the room. His sword clanged on the floor near their bed. Another clatter followed. Two more shiny dirks dropped to the ground.

Sarah sighed. Attempting to seduce him had been another bad idea. The jerky movements as he snuffed the candles told her so. That and the lack of conversation. Just as he did most nights since the night Eunan had wreaked havoc on their lives, Jamie turned his back and tossed aside the swath of plaid that covered his chest. Sarah's hands twitched as he stripped off his homespun saffron shirt. In the moonlight, his back shimmered, muscles rippling, the thin scar that ran from his left shoulder to his waist a stark white line. She'd stroked that scar with her fingers more times than she could count.

She would only have one more chance to touch him.

Her bare feet whispered across the floor. Unlike the cavern, the stone was warm, heated by the fires on the lower level. He tensed even before her hand made contact and flinched when her palm settled.

"I'm not a saint, Sarah." Voice strained, his head dropped and his entire body convulsed. "Why do ye test me like this?"

"I don't want a saint." Her hand smoothed over the warm muscles and followed the ridge of each shoulder blade. Hard and warm, the skin undulated beneath her fingers, alive and as precious as gold. She laid her cheek against his back. His heartbeat hammered, and pine and whiskey filled her nostrils. She drank in the intoxicating mix. "I want you, Jamie. Just once."

He trapped her arms as they circled his waist. Lacing their fingers, he lifted one hand to his lips. He didn't kiss it. He just held the fist against his mouth, as if to hold back words.

"Please, Jamie. I'll never ask for another thing."

His inhale shuddered through them both. "I can't." He exhaled, a long mournful breath. "I can't control what happens when your uncle gets here. But I can control myself. I'll not give him reason to doubt my honor."

"And what about me?" Her voice quivered, but she sucked in the weakness. "Do I ever get a say? All my life, I've been dictated to, punished when I disobeyed. Just once, I want control. Just once, I want to decide how I live my life. Even if it's only for a night."

"We can't." He twisted and took her in his arms, hands sliding up her back to pull her close. The evidence he was weakening lay heavy against her belly. "Tisn't just my life that would be forfeit. Your uncle's not known for mercy, Sarah. He's known for the opposite. If I take your honor, he'll exact his revenge on every man here."

"He won't. I won't let him."

Jamie's jaw hardened. "Ye won't be able to stop it."

"He won't know."

"Aye, he will. Even if ye can lie convincingly, he'll learn of it once you're wed."

"No, he won't." She looked him in the eye. "Jessica told me how to fake it. No one will ever know."

His hazel eyes widened, and his body went still. The hope that flared in his eyes sent a wash of relief through her. "Tis dishonest."

She traced a finger along his lips. "I don't care. It will be my sin, not yours."

His lashes swept down, and a shudder ripped

through him.

"Please?" She slid closer until his prick reassured her he wasn't as opposed as he claimed.

"Jessica needs to be hog-tied." A finger traced along the lace shoulder strap, twisting it until her nipple pebbled at the strain. "She probably told you to cry, too, didn't she?"

Sarah giggled. "How did you guess?"

A sad smile stretched his lips. "Because that's how she makes Bryan do her bidding." His lips lowered, brushing lightly along hers. She sighed, then gasped as one hand palmed her breast. The other cupped her ass. "Kiss me, Sarah," he whispered. "Show me how much you want me."

Lifting on her tiptoes, she nibbled the corner of his lips. Heavy and warm, his hands lay unmoving, but heat radiated through her. When he still didn't move, she clasped his neck and dragged him closer. Pliant, he allowed her to move him, but did nothing to help.

Urged on by the memories of what she'd liked when he pleasured her, armed with the knowledge Jessica had imparted, she licked his bottom lip, tracing the outside curve. Aside from a slight quickening of his breath, it seemed to have no effect. Her own blood heated though, and she redoubled her efforts. Her tongue darted out, lapping along the inside edge of his mouth, then kissing the corner and slipping along the bristly line of his jaw. When she sucked the hollow in his neck, where his pulse beat, his fingers tightened on the curve of her rump.

Fire streaked from his fingers and settled in the juncture between her legs. She shifted closer.

"Help me, Jamie. I don't know what to do."

"You're doing fine." Rough and low, the words reverberated along the vein in his neck. He began to move though, his hand smoothing over her hip and ass, bunching the fabric so it scratched. Her skin quivered and her mouth moved along the indentation in his shoulder. She lapped at his skin, salty, with tiny golden hairs that tickled her tongue.

A shock of want shot from her nipple straight to her center as his palm rubbed over her sensitive breast. She gasped, and her head fell back.

"You're so beautiful." The awe in his voice made her ache. The longing in his hazel eyes stabbed at her.

She cupped his face, savoring the bristles and memorizing the line of his jaw. In the moonlight, he looked like sun-kissed silver. "I love you, Jamie." The words finally came, bursting from her tongue like the desire streaking through her, uncontrollable. When he stilled, breath catching, she repeated it and pressed her lips to his. He was her life, too precious to forsake and too dear to resist. She had no choice but to love him.

"Are ye sure, Sarah?" His voice was as gravelly as his unshaven cheek and sent a shiver through her. "Ye're naught just saying it? Because I did?" His hand gripped hers, so tightly it hurt.

She swallowed hard. He'd hate her when she left, would think she'd lied, but she loved him more than life. "More than I can say." More than she could ever show. Even a lifetime of lovemaking wouldn't be enough. How would one night suffice?

Trembling, her hands slipped down and fumbled at the knot of fabric at his side. With a swoosh, the plaid pooled at their feet. His fingers grabbed hers, holding her a hand's width away, but his head fell back. Air whistled through his nostrils, and his throat rippled, the pulse hammering.

She'd never been surer of what she wanted. She eased closer, then fell to her knees.

He gasped and tightened his grip on her fingers. "Nay, Sarah!" He stumbled, then locked his legs. His other hand tangled in her hair, dragging her head back and forcing her face up. Shock widened his eyes, bright with horror. "What are ye doing?" he rasped, gaze raking her face before scraping over her lace clad breasts.

Hesitation and fear stole her voice. What if Jessica was wrong? He still hadn't agreed, hadn't done any more than they'd done before. Maybe he didn't want her mouth on him?

Her eyelids fluttered shut. "Please? I just want to love you." A sob shuddered through her, and his grip released. Her head fell forward, then her eyes widened. She had nothing to compare against, but the pulsing member before her looked huge. A tiny glimmer at the tip grew larger. Jessica said he'd not be able to resist if she put her mouth on it.

He grabbed her arms and hauled her up.

"God's teeth," he mumbled before his lips ground over hers. His tongue thrust in, hot and demanding. She responded, careening against him, lacing her freed fingers through the tangle of hair at his nape.

Suddenly, his hands roamed over her. They dragged the nightgown up, curling along her hips and waist, forcing the hem up over her ass. Hunger and heat trailed behind, and a whimper of need split the quiet. Then her breasts were on fire. Need snaked along her neck and up the length of her legs. His erection probed at her, coaxing quivers of heat from her core. When his fingers slipped between her thighs a gush of need filled her. Her legs gave out, no longer under her control.

He lifted her, hands slipping over her ass and levering her up by her thighs.

"Wrap your legs around me, *aingeal.*"

His mouth laved the curve of her jaw then returned to her mouth. She obeyed, and his hands roamed over her back, trapping her while his lips trailed liquid heat over her face and neck. Cool air washed her back, increasing the moist heat where his cock pressed against her softness. She gasped at the cold hard stone against her hot skin.

She glanced over her shoulder and tensed. White stone gleamed, circling a hundred feet in the darkness. She clutched his shoulders.

"Don't worry. I won't let ye fall."

Her fingers bit as one of his arms slid away. She jerked. A smooth hard knob caressed the folds where she bled every month.

Her body clenched. Jamie's arm clutched her while his mouth roved along her mouth and neck.

"Relax, *aon bheag.* Twill only hurt for an instant."

Jessica had told her the same thing, but suddenly, she didn't believe it. Her body did though, because when he nudged his hips forward, her insides unfurled. Warmth spread up, and hunger raced to meet it.

His eyes glowed as he gazed at her. She didn't remember the nightgown coming off, but her skin shone as white as the tower. Her breasts ached as his gaze lingered on them. She closed her eyes. The love in his eyes hurt.

"Love me, Jamie."

An instant later, he thrust, then stopped. Her brow furrowed, waiting for the pain.

"Are ye all right?" He didn't sound as if he were. He sounded like someone had speared him in the side again.

"Yes." It was a lie. Something was missing, something she needed. A tiny throb increased the sensation, spearing her core.

Jamie's head fell against her forehead, vein hammering. Another tiny jerk of his hips told her why.

"I need to move, Sarah." Strangled, his voice was so hushed she barely heard it, and he gritted his teeth and waited.

She cupped his cheek and touched her lips to his. Tight with strain, she licked the tension away and gave in to her instincts. Her hips rose, and she relaxed her legs.

He sank into her. "Heaven, lass. Ye feel like heaven."

With a gasp, she fell back, straining. A feeling of fullness flooded her. She pushed toward it. So close she sensed it, still it eluded her.

Carefully, he pulled away. His lips found her nipple, sucking in rhythm with his hips. Fire raced through her. She moaned.

Then he filled her again. Her legs tightened in anticipation.

He paused. When she relaxed, he slipped out again.

"No." She clawed at his shoulders. His lips roamed over her hot skin, leaving paths of coolness wetness.

"Let go, Sarah." He kissed her brow and rewarded her with another thrust. Another wave of love flowed through her. She fell back against his forearms.

Again, he leaned into her, then pulled back, only to repeat it. Swirls of sensation built between her legs, yearning aches that ripped at her heart. She'd never again feel like this, like the world would burst if she didn't embrace it.

She lifted her hips. "Again, Jamie. Love me."

He pounded forward, nudging her against the window. Another shock shook her core with promises of tantalizing, tempting heat. She sobbed, sure she'd die soon. Her eyes opened. Above her, the stars bounced until she realized it was her head jerking from side to side.

"I need to go faster. I'm sorry, love." Without warning, he grabbed her by the waist and began to slam his hips into hers. Faster and faster, waves of pleasure spiked through her. The hunger consumed, push by push, until she could bear it no longer. With a cry, she sank her fingers into his muscles and clenched, hammering back until his face twisted with need. His mouth devoured her, swallowing her scream before it formed. Certain she was going to snap, she arched her back, and like an iridescent bubble of soap, she burst.

He too collapsed, but not until he pulled her into a tight embrace and slumped against the wall, chest heaving.

"Ye're mine, Sarah," he said, wisps of breath battering her. "I canna let ye go. Ever. I'll find a way. Or die trying."

Chapter Sixteen

Sarah picked her way through the trees as rapidly as possible, but the bushes seemed to have grown hands. With each step a holly or wild rose reached out and snagged her gown or a tree root snatched at her toes. The near dark only made it worse. She couldn't watch for treacherous plants and keep up at the same time.

She'd snuck out well before dawn, after one last lingering touch. As she'd arranged, Niall had been waiting at the pond entrance. They'd descended the rocky goat trail and slinked through the first two layers of Bryan's men. Once, they'd nearly been discovered, but Niall had bluffed his way through while Sarah crouched behind a tree. She'd had to listen as he lifted his kilt to prove his assertion he was "takin' a leak". The men had talked while urine streamed inches from her skirt. After a few minutes of bawdy gossip about someone named Gwen, Bryan's man had slapped Niall on the back and returned to his post.

Now, Niall stood near a fallen tree and waited. His nondescript face scowled, mouth drawn at the corners. As she rushed forward, he turned his face upward. The predawn twilight had given way to a cloudy gray day.

"We should have been further along." Fingers locked on her elbow, biting into her flesh. Brown eyes raked her front and lingered on her neckline, like maggots burrowing into her.

She raised her chin and stared back boldly. She was doing her best. If it wasn't good enough, so be it.

"Ye should have worn the breeches." His hand dropped away, and he set off again. Huge strides rustled the underbrush. Within minutes, he chewed up the distance. Sarah hurried behind, labored breath forming puffs of mist with each step.

How far did they have to go?

It didn't matter. The rest of her life meant nothing. She'd sacrificed it so the man she loved might have a chance at the life he wanted.

She lowered her eyes to the ground and trudged forward.

Soon, her leg began to complain. The constant slips on roots and wet leaves sent arrows of pain into her knee. Unused to trekking through the woods, the muscles grumbled. The pace was grueling, and Niall rarely stopped to wait for her. She'd had no breakfast, either, so her stomach added to the cacophony of discomfort.

After they'd walked a good three hours, Sarah spied a fallen tree. Covered with moss, the fallen oak made a comfortable seat as she dropped onto it.

Niall continued to walk, sticks snapping as his feet pounded at them until he realized she'd stopped.

"What are ye doing?" He stomped back.

"Resting." She pulled a handkerchief out and wiped at the sweat along her neck. "They'll find us soon enough." She inhaled. Juniper and pine filled her nose, overladen by the scent of damp earth. It reminded her of her uncle. He'd always smelled like the outdoors.

"We have to keep going." Niall reached out to grab

her elbow again. She jerked her arm away, slapping him.

"Why did you do it?"

"Do what?"

"Betray Jamie." She wasn't sure it had been him. Most of her plan relied on instinct, as did her suspicion. The men hadn't figured out who told the Mitchells about the tunnels. Jamie, Bryan, and Malcolm had spent hours trying to figure it out. Ramsay was the only suspect, but Jamie didn't believe it was him. But they didn't know about her conversation with Niall, about how he'd tried to undermine Jamie. None of them noticed how Niall watched her or how every now and then his eyes narrowed when he glanced at Jamie.

"I dinna betray him," he said, but his eyes flitted away, and his face flushed.

"I suppose Mitchell just magically stumbled into the caves. And Gavin and Evan slit their own throats."

"Get up." Niall's jaw hardened, and he reached for her arm again. "We need to go."

She smacked his hand away. "You go. I'm hungry, and my leg hurts. And I know you're taking me to them. Not my uncle."

Niall blinked then stared. A second later his brows lowered. "Your uncle's just like him. He can't save you. He's too busy talking."

She swallowed her retort. Everything hinged on her uncle, according to Malcolm.

She wished she knew why. What did Malcolm know that she didn't?

"Why, Niall?" She slumped forward. She'd hoped she was wrong, that she'd misread him. Even as she'd asked him to get her through the layers of protection, some small part prayed he'd surprise her. "Why do you hate Jamie?" Was it because of his sister?

"I don't hate him. He isna worth hating."

"Then why? Why betray him? Doesn't it bother you? What they did to Rory?"

Niall's tongue slithered out to wet his lips, and he spun away. "Rory wasna supposed to die. They promised." His shoulders heaved, then he straightened. "It's Jamie's fault, not mine. He should have given up, like he always does."

Jamie couldn't have exposed her. He hadn't known where she was any more than Niall.

"Jamie would do anything for you, Niall. Can't you see that?"

"He wouldna." Niall began to pace tiny circles that snapped the twigs beneath his boots. "He's a coward. Always has been. He should have killed the men who slaughtered his clan." Niall's knife came out, hand wrapped around it as if he planned to use it. "Your uncle would have. I would have."

Would he? Sarah cocked her head. Niall had always struck her as kind and gentle, except when he stared at Jamie's back. Jamie always partnered him with Ramsay or Logan for guard duty. She'd never asked why. She assumed it was because Niall preferred the bow and arrow over knives. But she'd heard tales about Ramsay and Logan's bravery from Rory and none about Niall. Niall had volunteered to stay in the tunnels with her, too. She'd thought it nothing but kindness.

"He should have fought for you, not hidden you in a dark hole." Niall spun around, and his eyes softened. He dropped to his knees before her, the dirk falling, forgotten, into the folds of her skirt. "Come away with me, Sarah. We'll go someplace safe, disappear where no one can find us. I'll marry you, and we can have bairns with your golden hair. I'll never leave you, like he will."

He'd said the same things before, in the tower, when he asked her to go away with him. Talked of marriage and bairns and his sister, Brianna.

"It wasn't just Brianna he left, was it?"

Niall's face melted with anguish. "He leaves them all. He uses them, then discards them. And they never want anyone else."

She cupped his face in her hand. "Did she know you loved her?"

He fell back onto his heels as if she'd slapped him. His eyes hardened, and he bounded to his feet. "Of course, she knew. She didn't care. Ella only wanted him."

She heard a rustle and a snap behind her. Out of the corner of her eye, she saw a dirty green tartan slip behind a tree.

"Did you ever actually tell her?"

His face twisted with fury, but he didn't have time to answer. Sarah squeezed her eyes shut as a blade winked and a shadow lunged. She didn't hear him fight back. After a strangled gurgle and a thump, he went quiet. The sharp scent of blood turned her stomach, and an instant later, the nauseating scent of garlic suffocated her.

****

"What do ye mean, she's not here?"

Jamie halted on the last step. His eyes scanned the great hall, the sliver of sunlight coming through the hole in the ceiling nearly blinding him. Men sat on the floor and around the hastily constructed table, lounging or mending tack or weapons. Jessica lumbered about, her stomach bulging beneath layers of green tartan, her hand rubbing the small of her back while Bryan and Malcolm stared at him, brows furrowed.

"We thought she was upstairs with you. Are ye telling us she isna?" Malcolm pushed away a trencher filled with crumbs. Bits of food clung to his beard as his head swiveled.

Jessica's restless footsteps ceased, and the clatter of tools died away.

The knot of unease that had formed in his stomach when he woke tightened.

His gaze bounced from man to man, ticking off the names. Carson and Irving were still on guard duty. Logan and Ramsay both sat at the table, half-eaten oatcakes in front of them. As he scanned the room, Drew walked through the door, bucket of water in hand.

He'd woken earlier. Sarah's hand had stroked his arm. She'd whispered something about needing the privy and promised she'd be right back. His gut clenched.

She'd stroked his brow. And he'd fallen back to sleep.

Frantic now, his gaze flew over the scene. Ned stood up, scowling, and the rattle of pans told him Jock was in the kitchen. As his eyes passed over Jessica, his gut heaved. Her flaming red hair flowed over her shoulders the way Bryan preferred it.

"What did ye tell her?" he demanded.

She whipped around. "Nothing." A red flush betrayed her. "At least nothing to worry about." She chewed her lip, and a knife appeared in her hands.

"Ye need to have a talk with your wife, Bryan." He believed her. "About minding her own business." Jessica had helped Sarah destroy his last bit of self-control, but she had nothing to do with Sarah leaving. He'd thought Sarah's urgency was because she wanted him as badly as he wanted her. And she did. But now, he suspected it was more. She'd been saying goodbye. But why?

Bryan's dark green eyes flitted between his wife and Jamie. "Aye. But first, I think we need to find your woman." He levered his girth up from the table.

Malcolm bounded up as well.

"Where's Niall?" Malcolm's voice deepened, and he strode toward the kitchen.

Who cared? Sarah was gone, and the hole boring into his heart widened with each beat.

Why would she leave?

Malcolm's voice hammered at Jamie, but he couldn't focus. His mind replayed the time since they'd found Sarah. Every word, every gesture, every minute, drummed through his brain. The curve of her lips at her first hesitant smile. The joyous lilt when Rory had tried to scare her with a caterpillar. The flush of embarrassment when she told him it was all right he was deformed.

He squeezed his eyes shut and skipped over it. He bypassed the thoughts of her singing and sewing and mopping the floor. He concentrated on the bad times. There hadn't been many. She'd forgiven him for not reassuring her the day after he touched her, the night he lost his heart irrevocably. She'd never objected to being shoved into the dark, alone, into her own private hell when Mitchell's men hunted. They'd cried together when Rory died, and he'd heard the guilt in her voice, but he'd never imagined she would leave.

"Jamie!"

Malcolm grabbed his shoulders and shook him. Jamie's eyes shot open.

"You. This is your fault." His gaze punched the larger man. He shoved Malcolm's arms away. "She heard you. Yesterday. You and your god-forsaken scheme." The one where Malcolm suggested they use her to get inside Mitchell Castle.

He turned away, hands ripping through his hair. How could he have missed it? She thought herself spoiled and rebellious, when in fact she was the most generous person he'd ever met. Generous enough to sacrifice herself. For them. For him.

"Aye. That's what I was just saying." Malcolm didn't flinch or even look sorry. "She used Niall. I should ha' seen it when he asked to switch shifts with me. He hates patrolling in the dark." Malcolm's head rotated. "She's damn smart. Figured out who betrayed ye and used him. She has to know he'll die."

"God's blood." Jamie slammed his fist into the door jamb. The pain did nothing to stop the prickling in his eyes. "I can't do this. I can't lose her." Not after he'd just found her.

The familiar weight of a hand fell on his shoulder. "Then don't." Bryan's voice rumbled near his ear. "Malcolm's plan is a good one. We discussed it more last night. Ye'll have to fight. I dinna think ye can talk yer way out of this one. But twill be over quick. Tis just the timing that's risky."

Jamie swallowed and relaxed his fist. This was

why he relied on Bryan. He always saw the best way forward and never feared taking it. And Sarah had already set it in motion. She'd taken the choice away, but even if she hadn't, he would have fought for her.

"All right." He nodded his head. The lump slipped down his throat and lodged in his gut. "Tell me. What do we do?"

"First, we send word to Alexander," Malcolm said. "Then, ye do what ye do best. Negotiate. I hear the Devil's rather fond of souls. We've three amongst us. Do yer best not to sell all of them."

****

With no clear idea of what Malcolm's plan entailed, Sarah was left to fret. They'd locked her in the pigsty they called her room for a day, where she'd listened to hundreds of men pour in and out of the castle gates, their horse hooves pounding over the courtyard, urgent voices cursing and demanding. Eilidh had waddled in once, to pinch and prod and gloat, but no one else had come. They were waiting, Eilidh had said, for the roving preacher.

Sarah knew better. They were preparing for battle, a much more pressing concern than wedding her. Now, she found herself led through the dark, dank hallways of Mitchell Castle, just as dirty and unkempt as when she'd arrived all those years ago. The tallow candles still smoked and sputtered, and the guards once again chortled at her misfortune, but this time, she refused to cower. While not exactly a confident stride, she walked with her head high and eyes forward as they led her toward her future.

It wasn't the library doors they pushed her toward this time. Instead, they prodded her toward the cavernous great hall, a room she'd always dreaded. It was there that Hammond's men had always stared at her. It was where she'd watched her mother wed Hammond, and there that she'd felt Euanan's eyes on her.

How long before Malcolm's plan worked? Would her uncle help, or had she doomed herself?

An unnatural hush hovered over the hall as they approached, their steps muffled by the height of the ceiling, and Sarah clutched at her skirt. Men milled in the smoke-filled space, their black and blue kilts indistinguishable from one another, but no one uttered a word. Even Edgar, who had taunted her unmercifully that last time, remained silent. The crowd parted as they stepped into the room, and Sarah moved as gracefully as her leg allowed. Terrified, she stared straight ahead, focusing on moving one leaden foot in front of the other.

"You always did have a penchant for making trouble, Sarah."

Her gaze snapped toward the familiar voice. White-haired with bushy brows atop piercing blue eyes, her uncle stood beside Hammond. Tall and elegant in a snowy white shirt and his typical muted blue tartan kilt, the sight of him sent a surge of hope through her.

Flustered, she dropped into a clumsy curtsey. "Uncle."

He strode forward, each booted stride hammering. A meaty hand turned her face from side to side while he scowled. "You seem none the worse. Despite your escapades. But you've put me in a bit of a pickle, lass."

Unsettled, Sarah's gaze jumped from her uncle to her stepfather. Alexander looked grim, his eyes darker than usual, and she'd rarely seen him without a smile. Hammond looked smug, cruel lips stretched and eyes bright with triumph.

"In what way, Uncle?"

"I've been told you've dishonored your name."

Sarah shook her head. He couldn't know that. Only she and Jamie knew. And maybe Jessica. But even she could only guess.

"No?" His brows rose. The hold on her chin tightened, his fingers pressing until tears pricked her eyes. His eyes bored into her. "Are ye telling me the MacIan lied?"

Alex stepped back and waved a hand.

A door opened, and chains clattered. Four burly men clad in Campbell colors dragged two figures forward and tossed them at Alex's feet.

Sarah gasped, and her heart stopped.

Jamie and Malcolm slumped, arms fastened around bars that distended their shoulders. Dried blood darkened Jamie's golden locks, and Malcolm's left eye glared at her, the right swollen shut. Both men's clothes lay in tatters, their kilts muddied and bloody. Purple and green bruises colored their skin.

Her stomach lurched.

Surely, this wasn't part of the plan. Had the plot been discovered?

"Do I need to kill him, lass, or not?"

She raised stricken eyes to her uncle. He stared back as emotionless as the wall behind him.

What should she say?

"The truth, Sarah. Did ye lie with him or not?"

Sarah's fingernails bit into her palms. "No." The lie caught in her throat, but she forced it out.

His lips thinned into a sneer. "I see some things haven't changed. You never could tell a decent lie." He weaved between Hammond and Euanan, his gaze taking them in before he turned and ambled toward Jamie and Malcolm. When he reached Jamie, his hand lashed out and ripped Jamie's head back.

Sarah's breath hissed. Jamie glared at Alex with hate in his eyes, his chest taut while the bar tore at his shoulder sockets.

"Did you hope to gain her fortune, MacIan? Because you won't. She gets nothing unless I approve her choice. Just as her groom gets nothing unless she weds him of her own free will."

Alex released Jamie's hair. Jamie's head fell forward, but his eyes locked on Sarah. Pain-filled but steady, his gaze stroked her face.

"Which leaves us all in a quandary." Alex's shiny black boots circled the group. Hands behind his back, he ambled in and out of the onlookers as if strolling through court. "You see, I had big plans for my niece. I dreamt she'd wed a king or a duke at the least. Someone with influence, who could call up hundreds of men when needed." He continued to wander amongst the group while he talked. "Instead, I find she's ruined. Not just once, but twice."

Alex stopped in front of Hammond. A needlelike dirk appeared. He fingered the point while he glared at the smaller man. Hammond shrank before him. Although garbed similarly, the white of Hammond's shirt looked gray and his tartan dirty and coarse, almost black. Even his boots looked scuffed and worn compared to her uncle's gleaming leather.

"Tell me again, Mitchell," Alex said, tapping her

stepfather's shoulder with the tip of the stiletto, "how many men you command."

Hammond thrust out his chest. "Two hundred and thirty."

Alex's gaze circled the room. Sarah watched his gaze pause every so often. Then she followed suit. Devoid of tables, the room was large enough to hold a hundred or more men. It was full, men in varying shades of blue and green plaid milling amongst one another.

"And you thought you could hold me off with that?"

"Mitchell Castle's never fallen." Hammond exhaled, and his eyes darted away.

Alex shrugged and returned his dirk to his belt. "I'm aware of that. But the Campbells have never desired it. Just as I never agreed to your marriage to my sister." A rustle of movement broke out. Hammond's men clustered together, edging toward Hammond and Euanan. Seemingly unafraid, Alex turned his back on the man.

Nearly two-thirds of the onlookers had moved to show support of Hammond.

"But..." Alex rubbed the bridge of his nose and turned back toward Hammond. "What's done is done and cannot be undone. All we can do is make the best of it."

Alex smiled and turned his gaze on Euanan. Sarah's stomach cramped. Restless, the pockets of men began to shift. From the corner of her eyes, Sarah saw her uncle's lighter green tartan begin to weave amongst the darker dirtier groups.

She gnawed her lip and looked at Jamie.

Defenseless and bound, the only thing between him and Hammond's men was the two Campbells who had manhandled him. Large and toned, both held wicked looking axes and likely had at least one dirk in their boots.

Her gaze floated toward Malcolm. His undamaged eye closed, and his lips curled. Arm muscles flexed, and the entire bar rattled before one of her uncle's men smacked him with the blunt side of his ax.

"You," Alex said as he paused before Euanan, "are definitely not what I would have chosen for my niece." Alex's fingered the edge of Euanan's cravat. "But I suppose you're presentable enough. And your father's forces aren't meaningless. Tis better than selling her to some backwater baron who'll only want her to mother his brats."

With a sigh, Alex stepped back, then cocked his head at the man standing at Euanan's right shoulder. "What do you think, Duff? Is your friend willing to settle for a wife who's had another man? Would you?" The dirk reappeared, the tip held point up with one finger as he considered the man.

"Would depend on whether she's willing. You said her fortune is considerable. Twould make her more palatable if it came with her."

Alex's chin and brows lifted. His dirk pointed at Duff. "There is that." He spun away and locked eyes with another Mitchell man. His chin gestured at the man. "You, what's your name?"

"Wade, Sir."

"Did you encounter my niece while she was here?"

Wade's throat rippled. His gaze slid over Sarah. She remembered him. He'd watched her many times.

His eyes paused on her leg, then slipped back toward her uncle.

"On occasion, sir. But she never said much to anyone."

Alex's head rotated between her and Wade. "She always was a tad quiet." He tapped the knife tip against his fingers and paced before the man. "Did she cause any trouble? Do anything to disgrace herself?"

"No, sir. She was always a lady. She looked lonely and scared but was always polite."

"Would you marry her? Ruined as she is?"

"Twould depend on whether she wanted me."

The knife paused in midair, and Alex scrutinized him. "So, you would marry her for her money, but not otherwise?"

"Nay. I'd marry her if she wanted me, but not if she dinna." He shot a weak smile at her.

A snort from behind the man drew Alex's attention.

"What? You don't think my niece would have Wade?"

The man's lips curled with derision. "She probably would. A cripple like her doesn't have many choices."

"Very true." Alex nodded sagely and flicked the knife in his direction. "I tend to forget that."

Sarah swallowed her gasp before it made a sound. Hope filled her. Was her uncle marking them?

Before she had time to consider, her uncle marched to a halt before her. Suspicious, one of the guards who'd led her in sidled up beside her. A meaty hand hooked on her arm. She jerked it away.

Fury flashed in Alex's eyes then evaporated. He leveled a disdainful look at the man and waved the knife at him. "Are you afraid she'll run away again? I assure you she'll do no such thing. Unhand her." He turned to the man on the opposite side. The knife waved again. "And you, back up. You smell like blood."

Both men shuffled their feet, but Hammond cleared his throat and gestured them away. Alex pinned her with his blue eyes.

"So, button…" His lips trembled at the pet name before stiffening again. "It seems we're at an impasse." His gaze wandered toward Jamie then returned to bore into her. "Hammond wants your lover dead, and Euanan wants your money. I want you married to someone who has something to offer. So what should we do?"

Sarah dragged in a breath. It was a game. One they'd played every time her uncle visited. When she was a toddler, it was for sweets. He'd bring three treats. He let her buy two, one for herself and one for her father, who always gave his to her. The price was negotiated. He and her father would ask for kisses and hugs in exchange for the candy.

As she got older, he'd bring other gifts. Always one was worth much more than the other two. The coin became activities, like a chess game or the right to go into town or stay up late. She'd learned that relinquishing her claim too easily never earned the coveted treat. Instead, her uncle taught her to look at what was on the table and who gained and lost the most. A deal that resulted in two of the three participants leaving with something of value gained her more. In the end, she'd always end up with all three treats, but only after he explained whether or not she'd made the right choice and why.

Here, the choice was easy. She didn't care if anyone else won what they wanted.

But her uncle had laid out the terms for her. He expected her to bargain. And he'd given her an advantage.

Never let your opponent know what you really want or are willing to concede.

"I'll never agree to wed Euanan." She let her eyes sweep the room, forcing her gaze not to pause when it passed over Jamie and Malcolm. Her uncle's men were outnumbered, but as she looked, she realized they weren't all Campbells despite their garb. Carson and Keith wore her uncle's colors and mingled with the larger Mitchell men. Even Ramsay had donned the muted Campbell colors.

"You'd rather watch your lover die?" Alex lifted his brows, a move he'd used when she was very little and made the right choice. He'd lower them when she made a wrong move.

No one would believe her if she said yes. She scrambled to find an answer they'd buy. One that wouldn't give away just how much the idea terrified her.

They didn't think her smart enough to play this game. They thought her a spoiled, useless cripple.

Threaten what they want.

Euanan wants money. Hammond wants Jamie dead. But he wants the Campbell connection more. That was what her uncle hadn't mentioned. It was probably what allowed him through the gate.

"No," she finally admitted, praying she was right. "I don't want anyone to die. But I'd rather wed a backwater baron than Euanan. At least then I'd have the life I'm used to." She pretended to shudder and grimaced as she looked at her muddied, tattered gown. "I cannot stand another minute in this god-forsaken country. The Scots are savages. The wool itches, and it's always cold. I want my pretty gowns back."

She lifted her chin and ignored the prick behind her eyes. "But I'll wed Euanan. If you let the MacIan live."

"Nay!" Hammond stomped to Alex's side. "I'll not let a wench dictate terms. He dies, and she weds Euanan. That was the deal."

Alex nodded, but his knuckles turned white around the hilt of his dirk. "That it twas. But is his death worth a fortune? Her father was very specific. If she doesn't agree, you don't get the money."

"Bah. Tis your word that will decide, not hers. If ye say she agreed, who will say differently?"

Her uncle's lips thinned, and his gaze flickered toward Jamie. "True. But twould be an advantage to have him and his laird beholden to us. The MacGregor's been a thorn in our sides for some time. Sparing his life"—he gestured toward Jamie with his chin—"should be worth a boon or two."

"Enough!" Euanan strode forward, scowling. "I know your game, Campbell. You hope to gain from both sides. But we'll not play. Either she weds me today, fortune and all, or the deal is off."

A heavy sigh deflated her uncle's chest, and his hand fell to his side. "I suppose it was a vain hope, anyway." He surveyed the room, his face creasing with regret, then he strode toward Jamie and stopped before him. As he stared at the man she loved, Alexander's face solidified in a way she'd never seen. His eyes darkened, his jaw as tense as stone. "You should have known better than to take what belongs to me. Now, I've no choice." His gaze shifted to Malcolm. "You, I'll spare. So you can spread word of what happens when one crosses the Devil of the Highlands." He spun and strode toward Sarah, every ounce of gentleness gone.

"Tis time, Sarah," he said as his hand locked painfully around her left arm, "to find out what it means to be a Campbell." Pain streaked up as he dragged her toward Euanan.

Then, just as suddenly, her uncle jerked her away. Her weak leg buckled, and she lurched. Someone stepped between her and Euanan and steel flashed.

A bloodcurdling scream erupted. Blood splashed, spattering her face, hot and metallic smelling. A hand shoved her, pain exploding in her knee, and a body smashed into her. Hampered by her skirt, she scrambled to rise, but a heavy weight held her down.

Around her, the sound of swords clashed, and yells filled the room. Shrills of pain assaulted her ears, and a body dropped beside her. Wide-eyed, a horrified face gazed up, a river of blood gushing from the thick beard.

She shrank away, one hand uselessly attempting to hold back a cry. An arm snaked about her waist, and she shrieked. While hammering uselessly at the iron hold, her feet kicked the floor until suddenly she sailed through the air.

Breath whooshed as she collided with a rock-hard body. A shout arose, and a familiar voice sounded in her ear. "Get behind me, lass."

Malcolm shoved her back. A glint of steel streaked above her head, and she ducked. Another huge form wedged its way between her and the blade, a glimpse of familiar plaid covering its back. Gasping, she glanced around. A circle formed. Carson slashed at two frenzied Highlanders and two other men wielded an ax and a claymore, their expressions grim and deadly.

Nearby, her uncle, eyes blazing like blue lightning, stabbed at Euanan. Euanan, who flailed a wicked looking, bloody blade, lost ground with each measured thrust, his blows too wild and frantic to counter the steady determination in her uncle's face. As she watched, Hammond's men hesitated, some throwing their arms down and running while others died, their weapons clanging to the floor as screams broke off mid-breath.

Further away, in a tight cluster of hulking forms, Hammond jabbed at the air, a look of terror darting with each move. A ring of grinning Highlanders crept toward him, inch by bloody inch, as bodies dropped beneath their feet. Sarah watched for a heartbeat, then swiveled her head further, searching.

When she found him, her heart stuttered with relief. Like Malcolm, Jaime stood shoulder to shoulder with familiar Highlanders alongside the two Campbells who had dragged him into the room. Few stood before their slashing weapons. A puddle of slick red liquid and fallen bodies littered the floor before him.

A piercing scream rent the clangor of battle, and Sarah's head snapped toward it. Euanan rushed at her, blade arced above his head. Spittle bubbled from his lips, and his eyes blazed with hate. Hers widened as the steel winked above her head.

Carson's sword slashed up, clanging. Euanan's plummeted, the edge biting Carson's forearm, then clattered to the floor. A second later, Euanan's torso slammed into her, and a flood of warm wet liquid soaked her. Paralyzed, Sarah stared into his eyes. Blank, black points, they flared with shock, then dulled as a pink froth bubbled from his mouth.

With a scream, she shoved him away. He tottered, then thudded to the ground. She shrank back, staring at the lifeless face gazing at her.

"Mitchell!" A familiar sounding bellow snapped her head around. Jamie shrugged off a bloodied plaid then stepped toward a knot of men surrounding her stepfather. Sweat dripped over his honed muscles, every trace of the defenselessness he'd played at gone. A channel opened before him, men falling back as he stomped forward.

The last of Hammond's attackers dropped back, dragging in deep breaths, as if Jamie's bellow had been a command, until Jamie stopped. Cold, unforgiving hate glared at Hammond.

"You're a feckless bastard, Mitchell." Jamie pointed his blade, far enough away that Hammond straightened his spine and growled. "Slaughtering women and children. Did ye hide in the forest, waiting until I'd left? Or did ye strike in the dead of night, taking out the guards, so ye could butcher defenseless men and women while they slept?" Jamie's head shook, bloody sweat spraying. "We never did anything to ye. Never threatened ye, never even had words. Why would ye slaughter an entire clan?"

"Why?" Hammond's laugh crackled with scorn. His sword slashed the air. "Because we could. The MacGorans had no allies, no power, no reason to be." He cast a furtive glance at Alex and frowned. "Ye couldna even see what little ye did have. Ye could have been the Campbell's bard, had the strength of their name to shield ye. And ye turned it down. For what? For a woman?"

A strangled sound of fury bubbled in the air. Jamie lunged forward. Hammond's eyes widened. Jamie jerked his arm, and Hammond's blade spun up, then crashed to the floor. A boot trapped the metal, and Jamie's sword tip pricked the jowl below Hammond's chin. "That woman," Jamie spat, jaw clenched, "was named Joan. And she was worth ten of you. She loved me. A joy you'll never understand."

Hammond swallowed, and the next sound was more of a gurgle than a laugh. "Love is a weakness." His gaze flitted toward Euanan's body, and his face twisted. "It creates nothing but trouble. Unmans you." His chin lifted, and he turned a stony regard toward Jamie. "Go ahead, MacIan. Kill me. You want to. I see it in yer eyes. Or aren't you man enough?"

Jamie's brows lowered, and his nostrils flared. Then he lowered his arm and stepped back. "No. I won't kill you. I'm going to let you live with your failure. You can finish your life knowing that in the end no one loved you and no one respected you. You'll never again be spoken of except as the man who lost Mitchell castle." To punctuate it, Jamie scanned the room's massive space, then turned his back on the man who'd foolishly allowed them through the gates.

As his gaze landed on Sarah, the cold, hard lines melted, replaced by a look of anguish. A sob split the air, and she tried to move, but her limbs refused.

With a grunt, her uncle shoved Jamie aside. "MacIan may not be willing, but I am." A razor thin rapier sliced through the air, and a scream erupted. An instant latter, the sound stopped, and a thud echoed.

"No one holds a Campbell hostage and gets away with it."

After wiping the blade on his tartan, Alex grimaced at the body, then slid the blade into its sheath. He glanced at Jamie then rotated his gaze toward Sarah.

"Well, lass, are ye going to just stand there gaping? The man sold his soul to save ye. Twould be a sin if ye dinna want him."

Chapter Seventeen

Two months later, Sarah woke early. The fire had long burned to coals, and the faint glow the Scots called gloaming had just begun to brighten the room. Outside the pair of woodcocks fluttered back and forth amidst the shrill chirp of two hungry nestlings. A cool breeze tickled her back where the plaid had slipped, but she wasn't cold.

Careful not to wake him, she slid her hand along Jamie's chest. Even now she felt as if she were dreaming. After the nightmare of that day, her uncle and his men had descended on MacIan castle. They'd shored up the remaining defenses, restored the bulk of the timber skeleton within the walls, and celebrated her union with Jamie.

After much discussion between her uncle, Jamie, Bryan, and the surrounding clans, an agreement was reached. Jamie and his clan vowed to never raise arms against anyone, rescinding his longstanding oath to the MacGregor. In hopes of forging a more lasting peace amongst them, Jamie would travel from clan to clan during the summer months and share the gift of his song. In exchange, the Campbells and MacGregors promised defense against anyone foolish enough to threaten the young clan. Once word went out, a steady stream of peace-minded families had begun to arrive, ready to work and contribute to the idea of an existence without war.

Jamie's dream was a reality. And in some small way, she had a part in it.

As her hand smoothed the ridges of his chest, the well of love within her spiraled out. Like a pool of water, it rippled at the slightest touch, overwhelming her with the faintest smile, the whisper of his voice, the mere thought of him.

When he shifted restlessly, she snatched her hand away, but like lightening, his hand lashed out and grabbed her wrist.

"Do ye never sleep, lass?" He tugged until her length draped over his, his hands stroking her back, then her ass. "Tis barely dawn. And ye had yer way with me but hours ago. If ye keep this up, ye'll cure me before my third decade."

She laughed and wiggled her hips. Evidence of his lie throbbed eagerly. "I don't believe your affliction is curable. Not easily. At least I hope not." She sighed as their mouths met. Her lips tingled, still raw from their earlier passion, but this time the kiss was gentle and sweet, his tongue leisurely exploring with a pace matched by his fingers.

"Twill take a lifetime," he murmured between sips. "And ye'll be old." His teeth nibbled the corners of her mouth. "And still, ye'll make me stiff as a rock."

His hips lifted, and Sarah flinched.

"Auch, lass." His head fell back, and he gathered her close. "I've made ye sore again."

"No." Her head shook, her cheek flat against his chest where his heart thudded. "I'm fine."

"And still ye canna lie." Feather light touches stroked her back. They'd made love three times during the night, as hungry for each other as they'd been two months earlier. Each time had been just as intense as that night, as if it might be their last. "I'm sore. Ye must be as red and angry as a nettle infested plaid. Besides, ye'll wake the others if I love ye again the way I like."

Sarah smiled at the joke. More often than not, he had to stifle her screams, but the press of his lips negated any concern. When he pulled the plaid over her back, she snuggled closer.

"It's too quiet," she whispered.

She felt him tense.

"Aye." His chest rose in a long-drawn-out sigh. "And twill get quieter soon." He hesitated, his fingers slipping beneath her curls to massage the back of her skull. "Malcolm and Paddy are leaving soon. Bryan has a task he needs them to do."

"Oh." It would seem strange without them. "But they'll be back, won't they?"

"Mayhap. But one of them may not. Tis a clan up north. Bryan hopes to make a blood match. Paddy's to woo the Morgan's sister."

Her lips turned down. Jamie wasn't the only one who would miss them. She'd grown used to them. They were the family she'd never had.

You won't need them. Or me.

She shivered. Another flurry of wings preceded the hungry cry of the chicks and a wave of nausea swept through her.

Tis time. Tell him.

Sarah squeezed her eyes and tried to burrow into Jamie. She'd tried already. Twice. But every time she opened her mouth, it went dry with fear. What if she did something wrong? What if she made a mistake?

"Paddy doesna want to go. He's grumbling already, and I canna envy Malcolm. Twill be a difficult enough journey without Patrick's mood being black." Effortlessly, Jamie shifted, levering his body and rolling Sarah onto the mattress. With a sad smile, he traced a finger over her lips. "Malcolm's getting restless though. Twill be good for him, I think."

When she raised her eyes, a halo of light formed behind his head.

He frowned and rotated his head to see what made her eyes widen. "What's wrong, lass?"

She laid her hand on the dirk he'd lifted and lowered it.

"I have to tell you something." Fear flashed in his eyes, masked an instant later. It stole her courage, though, and she blurted out the less threatening announcement. "He's gone."

"Who?"

"Rory."

"I ken that, sweetheart." His eyes clouded, going darker.

"No, I mean he's truly gone." He hadn't been. Not completely. He'd hovered for a time, with Lady Aalis. "He told me to thank you. For taking care of him. But he couldn't stay. He missed his mam too much." The joy when he left had taken her breath away, but she feared telling Jamie, worried he'd think her mad.

But Jamie didn't look at her as if she'd lost her mind. He smiled. "Tis good. He deserves to be at peace."

"Lady Aalis is going, too."

He frowned at the tapestry they'd hung on the wall. "Are ye sure?"

204

"Yes." It stuck on her tongue, but she spit it out. "She says she's done here."

"Really?"

She nodded, the tentative hope on his face urging her to continue. "I wasn't sure at first. But she says it's true." She reached out and dragged his hand over her stomach. "You're going to be a father."

Her heart stopped for the instant his face froze, but when a sliver of sunlight shafted through the window and a grin blazed across his face, it lurched back to life.

"Thank the lord," he exclaimed and squeezed her so hard her breath caught. "Perhaps I can get some sleep now. Instead of having to swive ye three times a night." His laugh rippled up, as light and airy as her joy.

"Don't count on it." Her lips descended, then she paused to whisper, "I'm a witch, and I'll curse you if you don't keep me happy." Not as sore as she'd thought, she wiggled her hips.

"You're no witch," he responded. "You're my *aingeal*. My one and only *aingeal*.

About the Author

Terry Graham has been imagining love stories since she began playing with Barbie and Ken. In high school, she read Barbara Cartland along with Dickens, Austen, Asimov, and everything else she could get her hands on. After two careers, as a chemist and a computer programmer, she retired to try her hand at writing.

Terry lives in upstate New York with her cat Amber. She's divorced, with a grown son who makes it all worthwhile, and looking for a new Ken.

~*~

Visit Terry at

www.terrygrahamromance.com

Also Available
from The Wild Rose Press, Inc.
and major retailers.

A Matter of Manners

Shades of Sin Book One

By Terry Graham

Jeremy Wyles believes himself sterile. He's also a sadist and fears no lady would agree to marry him. When a woman shows up on his doorstep, pregnant and claiming to be his wife, he'll do whatever is necessary to ensure his dukedom has an heir. A loveless marriage in name only seems the perfect solution, but his disobedient duchess stirs his desire for discipline...and something more.

Irish rebel Kathleen "Katy" Brennan only seeks recompense from the husband whose cousin married her by proxy and left her with child. The bargain he offers is tempting. He'll claim her baby as his own, and she can become the grand lady she's always imagined. There's just one condition she's not sure she can live with. The delicious-looking duke refuses to touch her...ever.

Can Jeremy put aside the wicked urges that rule his life, or will Katy's rebellious spirit destroy his tenuous control?

Southern Rose

Gown & Dagger Seductions Book One

By Lily Bly

Rose O'Conner is a Confederate spy trapped among Union officers as the Civil War ends. When a Yankee from her past learns her secret, what is she willing to do to make him keep it?

Over the past year, Captain Grant Franks has searched for the alluring woman who stole his heart. When he learns she is a spy, will his dedication to the Union hold up against his desire for his Southern Rose?